SANTITIZA

Jonathan H Elliott

In memory of John Railton
A man who knew what it meant to guffaw,
and who did it in such style.

You brightened many a dull Dunbar-Edinburgh
commute.
Thank you for the encouragement, the wisdom,
and most of all,
thank you for the guffaws.

CONTENTS

1: MAILO (YESTERDAY)

When the third wave of the coronavirus pandemic spiked in Zambia, Evans was doing what Evans did best: nothing.

He was gazing at the condensation on his third beer of the day, contemplating the latest round of what felt like 27 arguments with one of his many girlfriends. He didn't like arguments. They were hard work, and Evans was not somebody who enjoyed working hard at anything.

Sam's Tavern was the premier destination for Evans and his drinking buddies. Whether it was the premier destination because it was the trendiest nightlife spot in the small town of Kafue or because Evans and friends had managed to get themselves barred from everywhere else was lost in the mists of time. However, one quick look around Sam's would be enough for an observer to conclude that the latter was the most likely reason.

There was just enough room for Evans and perhaps two dozen of his cronies, at the most. The walls were bare and cracking, covered only with what had once been white paint and peeling beer brand posters, with not a window in sight. The roof consisted of a corrugated metal sheet supported by wooden beams, from which a solitary light bulb dangled precariously on some rather suspect electrical wiring. The three most solid features in the room were an upright display fridge with clusters of two or three beer brands to choose from, the portly bar owner – Sam himself – and the bar, which Evans was perched beside.

A TV was blaring from a shelf in the corner above the bar. The country was in the middle of the election period; all the news stories seemed to centre on who had said what about whom. The only two topics that ever actually interested Evans – soccer and beer – seemed to have precious little chance of putting in an appearance.

He stretched his lanky body and glanced over at the TV. The reporter on screen looked a bit like Harold, his brother. His fellow drinkers all knew Evans had a brother. What they didn't know, despite their propensity for knowing more about your own life than you did, was that Evans and his brother were twins. Fraternal twins, yet so different in every way that even their own mother – God rest her – had wondered quite what had happened.

Evans was generally very slapdash in everything he did, from his appearance, with his partially tucked in shirt and mostly shaved scalp, to his cavalier attitude to life and work in general. By contrast, Harold was neatly pressed, sporting a carefully trimmed Afro that was two very precise centimetres and one right angle away from being OCD. Evans was chronically unemployed (and, frankly, unemployable); Harold was an important, successful businessman, at least in his own view. They didn't look even vaguely alike. Evans was tall, scrawny, with a long oblong face and eyes that told a tale of too many nights in the tavern; Harold was of average height, slightly rotund, and he had a circular face so lacking in charisma that it could easily be remodelled into a road sign.

Despite the election update presenter's appearance and general demeanour reminding him of Harold, Evans knew that the electoral process was not a topic to bring up in the presence of his brother. Harold could rant at length, with great energy, about many subjects and, until the arrival of coronavirus, politics had been a strong favourite. Ever since they were kids, it had been a constant source of amusement to Evans that his pompous, preachy, twin had never got the hang of his 'r' and 'l', continually interchanging the two. As a result, any discussions during the election campaign period included Harold making the bold pronouncement that he had a better understanding of "erections" than anyone else in the town. In fact, if Harold were to be taken at face value, nobody had "experienced more erections" than he had.

Evans turned his attention back to the TV, where a presidential candidate was now spluttering and blustering the way politicians do when asked to give a truthful yet precise answer. "Plundering with integrity can allow us to plan and build a great future for our citizens." At least that is what Evans thought had been said. It couldn't have been though, even if it was the unspoken manifesto of most candidates.

Evans had frequently thought that arguments with girlfriends were much like elections. It didn't really matter which box you ticked, you would still have to listen to a lot of talking the next day.

While Evans was contemplating the inside of Sam's Tavern and the elections waffle on TV, Harold had a red carpet function at a cinema to cope with. Why the cinema was even allowed to open, given the rapid escalation of coronavirus cases was beyond him. Nor could he understand why his bankers felt the need to announce changes to their product offering at the premiere of a Hollywood action movie. As far has Harold could tell, there was absolutely no connection between a bunch of intrepid heroes saving the world from nuclear disaster and a new type of long-term deposit account. After all, if the heroes didn't save the day, then any money in his bank account would be irrelevant; and if they did save the day, then he didn't really need to prepare for a disastrous future, did he?

Be that as it may, Harold knew that his banker

would be more likely to approve his next business loan if he attended the event so he smiled nicely at the banker, and, even more crucially, shook the hand of his banker's boss and told him what a wonderful chap his banker was and what wonderful service he was always given. Harold strongly believed he was an honest man, so he would utter phrases such as "the service is exceptional-" and then promptly develop a wheezy cough, which sadly would prevent him from concluding the sentence with "-ly bad."

He was proud of his business, a small hardware store along Kafue's main road. He had worked hard at building it up since he finished university. The loan he was applying for would allow him to do some renovations to it and make it significantly bigger, something he was sure the good people of Kafue would appreciate. He intended to include a raised private office with floor-to-ceiling windows from which he would be able to survey his empire, while sharing his wisdom on DIY with anyone who popped in to consult him.

Although most of Kafue's households survived on a fairly tight budget, and it was far from being the wealthiest town in the country, the need for building materials had given him a good income over the years. He regarded his store as the jewel in Kafue's shopping district, the brightest of the twenty odd small family run stores that were haphazardly plonked around opposite the newer strip mall that had been opened a while back. There was no doubt in his mind that his store was the star attraction of the town, perhaps even more so than the riverside bars or the boat cruise with its sunset views of hippos and the Kafue Bridge. After all, where else could one get the essential tools to improve one's home and essential wisdom to improve one's life at the same time?

It still astounded Harold how his twin had managed to fritter away the solid start he had had in life. True, their father had died young, but their grandfather had stepped in and made sure his twin grandsons were kept in line for as long as he could, until he too made the journey onward. Grandfather had scrimped together the money to send both of them to one of the best church-run boarding schools in the country, where Harold had ended up as class prefect, a role in which he lorded over his fellow pupils with more than a little pomposity. Meanwhile, Evans had usually been in and out of various mischievous escapades. Although Evans had never quite pulled in the best grades, he hadn't exactly failed, so it had been expected that both twins would go on to some form of higher-level education. Harold had gone on to study business whereas Evans had simply gone off the rails. Somehow, the long gap between Grade 12 exams and the start of the tertiary education terms evolved into a permanent gap in Evans's case. Moreover, with Harold having become increasingly disdainful of his brother, the difference in their education just further cemented the differences between the two.

For instance, when it came to the

forthcoming elections, Harold had analysed every candidate and their manifesto from a business and ethical standpoint. And he was always generous enough to share his detailed understanding with his customers. Why, one of them had even muttered to his fellow shopper that Harold was truly an anal-yst. He had put the pause down to the man's obviously inferior education. On the other hand, as far as Harold was concerned, Evans's approach to elections was simply to follow the best-funded candidates around, ever hopeful of getting something for nothing.

Harold would be surprised to know that Evans had actually been thinking philosophically about elections at the precise time he was also pondering this; he didn't really associate philosophical thought with his twin. He didn't really general give his twin credit for anything – except when it came to be being in the right place at the right time to benefit miraculously from it, which was what Evans seemed to excel in. If there was a free lunch or beer on offer, or someone had dropped a 50 Kwacha note, Evans somehow seemed to get the lion's share of the opportunity.

One of the challenges of being an important businessman and a pillar of Kafue's community was that, whether he liked it or not, Harold had to take frequent trips into Lusaka, Zambia's capital city. It less than an hour's drive from Kafue, but for Harold the worst part of the journey involved negotiating hazardous curves while trying not to lose his temper at what he saw as the recklessness of public service minibus drivers or the arrogance of the inter-city truck drivers. Often he was tormented by both on one trip, or even on the same curve.

Once he had arrived at the mall where the cinema was, he had donned his face mask and his beloved Harris Tweed jacket (an item of clothing that served as his trademark) and made sure he had his three essentials with him: a measuring tape (no self-respecting owner of a hardware store should ever be without one); "handi santitiza" (as he called hand sanitiser); and his inhaler, an essential that he wished wasn't quite so essential.

As he had made his way through the mall to the cinema, he had encountered two opposing groups of protesters. The first group, huddled closely together in a neat and tidy way by the roadside, were all masked up and armed with hand sanitisers and placards with legends like, "Mask up, stay safe", "Save our pipo", "No virus Yes jobs" and, rather bizarrely, "Free condoms". Harold was not clear as to the relevance of the latter. Still, at least they were all masked, even if they hadn't quite got the hang of social distancing. Ironically, the rather less civilised group protesting against lockdowns and restrictions were far better at social distancing – even if it was only because one needed to be a decent distance away from one's peers in order to have enough room to be able to throw a rock or bottle effectively.

Harold sighed heavily to himself as he

contemplated all this. So far, the red-carpet event had gone much as he had anticipated it would.

He had arrived exactly on time at the event, which needless to say, made him one of the first people there. Unlike his twin, Harold was a stickler for timekeeping. He firmly believed that Evans would be late for his own funeral, when that time came – he figured that the family would just be standing around waiting for his body to arrive.

This event would probably take even longer than usual to get going. Because it was election time, the invited dignitary would undoubtedly want to use it as an opportunity for a campaign speech, blowing more hot air into the already stuffy cinema foyer. Harold helped himself to a samosa from a tray held by a passing waiter, who was properly masked, thank God.

He held the samosa with a napkin in one hand while checking the time for perhaps the twentieth time since arriving. He had already praised the banker, and dutifully chatted to an assortment of business people and hangers on, and he really wanted to leave, but it was considered bad taste to leave before the dignitary had left. Harold pondered this for a bit. Was it really so rude to leave before the guest of honour if the guest of honour hadn't shown up by the time you left? After all, if you left before the dignitary arrived, then technically you hadn't left before them, because how could you leave a place before someone who had not yet actually proven that they were going to be at that place. He had just about cracked this conundrum in a way that would satisfy his sense of honour, when, much to his annoyance, he heard the mighty kerfuffle that heralded the arrival of the guest in question.

Harold had been surprised by the choice of guest of honour. As a general rule, bankers were risk-averse. They almost always chose a guest from the ruling political party, and usually someone who held a position that would perhaps allow them to nudge a rule or two in a direction that would benefit the bank's shareholders and profits. If the guest of honour also happened to have deep pockets and was willing to empty them in the general direction of the bank's vault, then that was even better.

However, in this case, the bank had opted for the somewhat unorthodox choice of an aspiring presidential candidate from an opposition party. Harold scratched his head and pondered this development. It wasn't just any aspiring candidate – it was the most socialist of them all. In fact, the candidate was so keen to prove his socialist roots that he was dressed in a sand-coloured uniform and cloth hat that would have had Fidel Castro asking to be introduced to his tailor. All that was missing from this homage to the Cuban icon was a beard; in TV images, the candidate had appeared to have the facial hair of a tweenager, and chubby cheeks to match. It created a very odd impression. Those thoughts aside, when Harold listened, he realised that the man was well-educated, articulate, and – to his surprise – he found himself almost stimulated by the speech, even if he was still in the dark about the connection between socialism, Hollywood heroes and the launch of a new type of interest-bearing chargeable deposit account. At least the candidate was wearing a mask. It was a start.

Then it was time to enter the cinema itself, and the Master of Ceremonies, having successfully told his one joke and mercifully run out of material, asked the guests to please form an orderly queue behind the guest of honour.

Harold sighed again. He had hoped that the movie in question would be of no interest to the politician, but it appeared that he had actually been looking forward to that part of the programme. There was nothing else for it, Harold would have to join the queue going into what he saw as a breeding ground for coronavirus, thus putting his valuable life at risk. He removed another face mask from the pocket of his Tweed jacket and layered it on top of the three he was already wearing.

It did seem like the cinema had made some attempt at thinking this through. Before anyone could enter the actual screening, they had to sanitise their hands and have their temperature taken to make sure that it was around 36-37 degrees Celsius and they were thus lacking a fever. In addition, only two people were allowed through the doors at a time. It did occur to Harold that it would have made more sense to do this before people had even entered the event space in the cinema foyer. However, he couldn't help it if he had more brains than anyone around him.

He was immediately behind a young couple in the queue. They clearly didn't understand the concept of social distancing as they were holding hands. Harold was clear; it was his civic duty to intervene and save them from potential disaster. He leaned forward and said loudly, "You are too close together! You need to stay safe!" He held out his hand sanitiser. "Use santitiza!"

The young man turned and stared at him. "We're in the queue for sanitiser, old man. And it's sanitiser."

"That's what I said, handi santitiza!" lectured Harold.

"San-i-tise," the young man said, emphasising each syllable.

"Leave him alone," his girlfriend interjected. She gave Harold a sympathetic look, uttering a "mwandi" of condolence to him. Harold was about to feel a bit better when she rather undermined the moment of empathy by adding, "They probably didn't have schools when he was small – look at his tuma jacket; he has just come for the free food."

Harold bristled as he tried to think of a comeback, and his hand went to smooth his Harris Tweed jacket, imported all the way from England. Not that that chit of a girl would even understand all that he had gone through to get it sent to Lusaka by his uncle in London. It was not an easy task to describe your size and tastes to a dim-witted distant relative sitting somewhere in the diaspora, especially one who spent most of each phone call telling you what was wrong with the country you were sitting in. After all, if his uncle was such an expert in what was wrong with Zambia, why was he not back there fixing it instead of sitting in a small centrally-heated flat in a grotty British suburb?

The couple reached the front of the queue, where the somewhat excitable cinema attendant helped them sanitise their hands. "Thank you, thank you, thank you" he said, with such enthusiasm that Harold began to think he had missed something. The attendant pointed the digital thermometer at the young man and read out his temperature. "Thirty-four point three degrees!", he announced, and turned to aim it at the young woman. "Thirty-four point three degrees! Also! You have the same temperature!" He beamed like a lighthouse. "What you have is so romantic!"

"What you have," muttered Harold to himself, "is a buggered thermometer." What was the point, he wondered, in having staff wielding thermometers when they had absolutely no idea what the correct temperature range was. Either the couple in front of him were in a state of hypothermia or reptiles so desperate to see a movie about nuclear annihilation that they had felt the need to disguise themselves as humans. Harold sighed and let the attendant wave the thermometer at him, wondering if the farcical situation the pandemic had brought about would ever really abate.

2: THIS DAY

Harold was seriously unimpressed with the welcome he received when he went to the bank the next morning. The Kafue branch was housed in a hostile-looking stand-alone single-story concrete rectangle with a shiny blue corrugated metal roof. There were cracks in the walls that the regular coats of white paint had done nothing to hide, tiny windows with metal burglar bars over them, and barbed wire everywhere. In fact, it could well have been used as the set for the prison the terrorist escaped from in the movie he had painfully endured. It wasn't just the fact that the physical realities were very far removed from the red-carpet, glitz and glamour of the launch; it was the overriding experience of a branch as badly maintained in personnel training as it was a building.

His bank had never been terribly adept at customer service, and the pandemic had only served to make them slower, surlier and generally more difficult than ever. Even the simplest of transactions had turned into a series of negotiations, caused by a mixture of COVID-19 fears and general bureaucratic ineptitude. For example, they had decided that the best way to increase staff safety was to cut opening hours by half. Of course, this did not reduce the number of people wanting to visit the bank – it simply meant that more people crammed themselves into the same space at a time. In fact, the branches were even more crowded than they had been before, because the safety procedures meant one had to spend even longer in there than ever before.

Harold sighed to himself over the short-sightedness of administrators and faced the scrawny, physically unthreatening security guard in an immaculately pressed uniform and blindingly shiny boots who was standing defiantly between him and the entrance to the branch. "I just want to get some money."

"I have to take your temperature" the guard repeated, not for the first time. "It is the procedure. Then you have to write your name in the book, apa so." He gestured at a large notebook and accompanying pen, the latter of which appeared to have been chewed thoroughly. "We are only allowing five people insides at a time" he added, clearly proud of himself for having remembered that detail. "This is what the rules are saying. Only five people to go through the door at one time. Everyone he has to sign in the book himself. And..." he raised his digital thermometer towards Harold's forehead, "...me to be am checking yo' temperature." Harold tried to avoid the guard's outstretched arm, but the more he tried to dodge it, the closer the guard moved to him. In response, Harold took another step back. This fencing movement continued for a few moments, by which time the guard's face had taken on a look of severe concentration. He appeared to be fighting the temptation to smack Harold in the face with his thermometer. After finally succeeding in getting close enough with his outstretched arm to Harold to get a reading, he sighed heavily.

Harold glared at him, perspiring mildly from the exertion. It was hard work avoiding close physical contact with an enthusiastic guard wielding a thermometer, especially when it was humid, over 25 degrees Celsius and one was immaculately turned out in a fashionable, though perhaps impractical, Harris Tweed jacket over his long-sleeved businessman's shirt. "When, exactry, did this start?" asked Harold, emphasising the wrongly pronounced *exactly*.

"Tomorrow" the guard explained.

"Yesterday, you mean" Harold corrected him. He couldn't help himself. He knew very well that mailo, the local word for yesterday, could be readily used for either "yesterday" or "tomorrow" or "later" (especially in the form of a casual commitment, such as when you were asking a plumber when they might deign to turn up and fix a dripping tap). Despite that, he always felt an obligation to correct people who were, in his view anyway, just plain wrong.

"Exactly" replied the guard, emphasising the

"1".

Harold took a deep breath. Normally this would have been the point where he vented his frustrations over time-keeping, and the question of how one could function in a society when one had no idea as to whether one was discussing yesterday, tomorrow, or some arbitrary, as yet undetermined, point in the future. It was simply infuriating, and one of the many small things in life that stressed Harold out and elevated his blood pressure.

Evans, inevitably, loved the word "mailo". He could tell a girlfriend that he would get her a gift "mailo", and then promptly proceed to avoid her for weeks. And yet, he wasn't lying, because he didn't generally lie; he simply applied the truth as he understood it. It wouldn't be his fault if by the time "mailo" finally came around he didn't have any money left for a gift; that was just the way life went. Mailo was also a great saviour when it came to responsibilities, he could proudly explain he had kept a promise, without necessarily having done it, simply by being a bit vague about its timing. When it came to such debates, mailo was simply a beautiful word. Evans had lost count of the times it had got him out of trouble and saved him from worrying unnecessarily about some pending problem; after all, mailo never came.

Harold was still debating whether to begin this pressing debate, when the guard pointed at his desk. "You can write in the book now."

Harold gave the guard a further glare, liberally

covered his hands in sanitiser and gingerly picked the pen off the desk. He was all too aware that as a strategy for disease control this was particularly ill thought through. Yes, the bank may have succeeded in having a list of everyone who went into the bank, which would be perfect for contact tracing in the event of a member of staff or customer testing positive for COVID-19. In doing so, however, they had clearly overlooked the fact that they were increasing the chances of the customers and staff contracting the virus, as every single person ended up touching the same pen. It was even mounted beneath a poster advising their customers to go cashless to avoid physical contact with surfaces. As a policy, it seemed like a self-fulfilling prophecy.

Harold scribbled something unintelligible into the book – he was of the opinion that he was far too important for lowly bank staff to have his contact details, and, sanitising again, walked into the branch, studiously following the lane and queue-spacing markers on the floor. He was perturbed to see that there were decidedly more than five people inside the branch – until it dawned on him that the guard had probably interpreted "only five people through the door at a time" quite literally and was letting anyone in provided that more than five people didn't try to enter at the exact same time.

It was a bit cooler in the bank, which was just as well, given the amount of time he was likely to spend queuing. Social distancing or not, Harold would have preferred not to stand in a line listening to irrelevant gossip. Despite the bank claiming to be the preferred bank for "serious" businesspeople, he never seemed to meet any of those in the queue – although, he had to admit a few individuals at the red-carpet event had caught his notice (and not just because of their physical bulk from too many long fine business lunches). They had seemed more like him, a serious man dedicated to building his life and career.

So it was only natural that the bank should have invited a person such as himself to their event, reflecting the value they placed on him as a "highly esteemed customer". Those were their words, not his. They used them each time they sent him an announcement about a change to branch operations. They always started "Dear Highly Esteemed Customer". He had doubts as to whether his twin was held in such high esteem.

Evans was simply a layabout. He couldn't begin to understand why his twin was never engaged in anything useful – his life seemed to revolve around shirking responsibilities and identifying means of depriving relatives such as himself of their hard-earned cash.

He knew his twin simply didn't see it that way. Evans thought he was highly industrious, and an international entrepreneur. No, scratch that, he thought he was an international philanthropist. One of his many sources of income was to separate the gullible around the world from the cash that they clearly had more of than brains. Evans believed that it was important to deal with the excess that the rich had built up by encouraging them to support one of his many not-quite-in-existence commercial ventures, and subsequently redistributing that wealth to far needier persons, such as his many different girlfriends and Sam, perpetually perched in his tavern.

In fact, Harold would have been surprised to learn that the bank much preferred Evans's moan-free business to Harold's whinging pedantry, especially as Evans earned them a decent revenue stream in in-bound money transfers, albeit from questionable sources. By contrast Harold nit-picked over every single charge the bank dared to levy on him.

About half an hour later, Harold was sighing heavily at one of the teller counters in the bank, adjusting his mask, when Evans strolled in and gazed around him. The sight of his layabout twin's bolshie, arrogant swagger and grinning mask-free face only made him sigh all the more. He turned back to face the teller in the hope that he might escape Evans's notice.

The teller had clearly been diligently bleaching her skin, but her choice of make-up left her looking pale and ill, rather than the bright attractive radiance she was aiming for. Harold never understood why women wasted so much time on their appearance – if they way they were born was good enough for God, and most of them seemed to spend all weekend in choir practice or at church anyhow, why was the look not good enough for themselves? It was really rather puzzling. The teller looked past him at Evans and winked, which went beyond puzzling into the realm of simply astounding. Harold could never understand how Evans appealed to so many of these women. Even his own wife Mercy had described him as a charmer.

"Bro!" Evans stretched out his hand as he spotted Harold.

Harold recoiled in fear, trying to put more space between them. "Evans. You are here?"

"Yes." Evans looked down at himself, as if he was checking. "It seems I am. How's it?"

"Fine, fine" Harold moved further back, almost falling over in his efforts to avoid Evans's outstretched hand. "Don't touch me, there's colonavilusi, don't you know?"

"Ah, but you are my brother, mweh!" Evans kept moving forward, causing Harold to stumble and fall. He put his hands down to support himself and touched the floor.

"Aaaaah!" Harold looked at his hands in horror. "Where's my handi santitiza?" He rummaged for his bottle, liberally covering his hands with sanitiser as he got back to his feet.

"Awe, Harold." Giving upon the hope of a handshake, Evans withdrew his hand and shook his head. "Bro! Awe." He paused, contemplating his next gambit. "How's Madam?"

"My wife," Harold bristled, "is fine." The use of

"madam" always niggled at him. He pointed at the floor markers. "Evans. You need to be standing there. Please, be serious for one time in your life."

The bank teller coughed loudly to regain Harold's attention.

"You're sick?!? You're coughing?!?" Harold panicked, his voice becoming squeaky. He started to step backward, before realising that would bring him even closer to the mask-free Evans. He almost shouted at the teller: "You should be home!"

The teller sighed loudly. "I'm not sick. I was trying to attract your attention."

"Then you are a fool," said Harold. "This is a pandemic!"

"You're an expert in that field, sir. I understand how you recognised it."

Evans laughed loudly, hoisted up his trousers, and tried to nudge Harold. "Bro, finish yo' business. Some of us have bars to get to."

Harold asked the teller for some cash, and asked Evans if he was mad. "Bars are closed, don't you know anything?"

"The doors are closed, but the bottles are ohhhhhhpen my friend!" Evans smirked with a wink at the teller. He wondered if he might find her at his favourite bar later.

The bank teller flexed her fingers and picked up a stack of notes. "Here's your money, sir," she said, enunciating the "sir" in a way that was clearly an insult.

"Have you disinfected it?" Harold asked,

trying to scrutinise the money from afar. "Are you sure it's clean? I only want fresh notes!"

"Yes, sir," she replied, the boredom evident in her voice. "Every note is washed in Dettol. That's what I spend all evening doing." She reached out to give the money to Harold, who was preoccupied with sanitising his hands again.

"No, no, no! Just put it there, I'll get it." Harold pulled a pair of disposable gloves from his pocket, and used them to pick up the money.

Evans stepped forward. "Harold, get on with it, man..."

"I am just staying safe!" Harold said, as he walked around Evans, giving him as wide a berth as the walls would allow. "I am not going anywhere near anything!"

"I'll come home later, your madam can allow." Evans laughed loudly at the evident fear on Harold's face as he scuttled from the bank.

3: THAT OTHER TIME

Once his banking chore chore over and done with, and another of the gullible had been safely parted from their cash, Evans was not quite sure what to do with himself. During election period, his normal source of employment, to use a very loose term for it, was to put in a personal appearance (as he saw it) in the crowd at political rallies. He was quite proud of his record, he had been a face in the crowd in newspaper photos on more than one occasion, and once, when the incumbent president was inaugurating a new set of streetlights, he had even appeared on the evening TV news. His attendance at the numerous Presidential openings of road infrastructure over the last few months had been so consistent that he felt it was high time the President named a street after him.

This might lead an observer to believe that Evans was a man of strong political convictions with a crystal-clear understanding of party politics. Nothing could be further from the truth. He did in fact have finely honed insights, but these insights were centred around which party would give him free t-shirts, beer and food, and when. He would happily switch allegiance and party colours from one day to the next. This practical approach to politics had served him well for many years.

Ukselela kwa kaba, or swapping allegiances depending on where the best reward was to be found was one of Evans's skills. He had crafted this ability to swap political loyalties, soccer teams, sides in an argument and even girlfriends to such a subtle level that even he himself sometimes forgot which side he was on at any given time. There was a deftness to being able to swap sides halfway through an argument, especially one in Sam's Tavern that might end up with the winner buying everyone on his side a round of drinks. This was even truer when you were the sort of kamu selela kwa kaba who could distract people from realising that you had, in fact, rather noisily been supporting the other point of view when the argument started. Evans took pride in the day when he had secured three successive free drinks during a local football match by enthusiastically changing his mind three times as to which team was playing better as the game went along.

Although the current lock-down and consequent restrictions on election rallies had somewhat curtailed his sources of free food, Evans was glad of the break. His last excursion had almost earned him a severe beating, which had made him marginally more self-aware than he had previously been. He had discovered perhaps that the fine art of ukselela kwa kaba was not always the easy deal he had thought it was.

It had all started much like any other rally day: get up; eat an early breakfast while tuning out the latest lecture from his live-in girlfriend; put on the campaign t-shirt for the relevant party (which invariably had the candidate's head blown up to an exaggerated size, usually with some equally inflated promise); and stroll down to the bus stop to join a rowdy bunch of cadres ready to lay down their lives for their candidate. Evans wasn't quite ready to lay down his life for any particular party, he knew, and although he would stand there and nod enthusiastically and shout "welle" whenever he was supposed to, he generally spent most of his time admiring the backsides of the women dancing energetically, with chitenges emblazoned with the President's face covering their ample behinds. Evans never quite understood why the President would gladly have his face on something people wore wrapped around their waist and sat on; he mused on how much time His Excellency's face spent sandwiched between large buttocks and minibus seats.

That fateful morning had been rather chilly, with the grey skies and cold July breeze that sometimes winds its way along the foot of the Kafue hills. Evans had thus decided to put a sweater over the obligatory campaign t-shirt.

As the minibus jolted, shook and snaked its

way south towards the next town of Mazabuka, where the rally was being held, the combined effect of a bus full of sweaty cadres and the approach of the noon-day warmth made him decide to remove his sweater.

He had just put his sweater on his lap and proudly puffed up his chest when he realised his t-shirt was the wrong colour. He'd worn the opposition's shirt! He dived towards the front of the bus at breakneck speed –it was probably the fastest Evans had ever moved – just as the others in the bus began to shout. Avoiding several swiping fists and others attempting to clutch at his shorts, Evans managed to force open the bus doors and jump out. As the bus was screeching to a halt, Evans was busy disappearing into the dense brush that lined the road and running flat out.

It annoyed Evans intensely that virtually everyone else on the bus was there for the same reason as him; it was how they made a living. The only difference between himself and the other passengers that day was that he blundered by wearing the wrong party's t-shirt. That mistake had made him firmly persona-non-grata with that particular party, and it had left him taking a bit of time to review his political allegiances – at least for as long as it took him to walk back through the bush to Sam's Tavern.

Evans patted the pocket that was full of the benefits of having parted another gullible relative from their money. As time had shown him that there were, perhaps, occasions on which he should be a bit more strategic in his hunt for the perfect balance between entertainment and earning some money, Evans realised he had two choices when it came to what to do with the rest of his day.

He could wander over to the construction site where his mates Bwalya and Mulenga were gainfully employed. Bwalya and Mulenga were both employed in two roles on the same site: one the foreman knew about, and a slightly less legitimate one that he was blissfully unaware of. Their legitimate task involved moving cement and bricks from the locked container into the melee of workers labouring away; their more profitable employment involved losing a bag of cement or some bricks here and there along the way, and sharing in the reward when a kind member of the community decided to clean up the mess they had accidentally made.

If Evans took the trouble to walk over the building site, he could see if there was any chance of some piece work, at least enough for a beer or two afterwards. This seemed to be a good idea, especially the last part. However, on reflection, as he was never a big fan of over-complicating his life, he decided to skip the walk and the piece work and go straight to the beer or two.

Running into Evans in the bank may have been an unpleasant encounter for Harold, but, later in the day, back in the relative safety of his own home, he realised he had got off lightly. Normally Evans would have taken the opportunity to try to talk Harold into investing in his latest amazing business opportunity. On every occasion that Harold had suffered his way through such discussions about Evans's schemes, it had always seemed to him that the opportunity would involve Harold contributing a significant amount of money to Evans's venture, and Evans making an equally generous contribution to the opportunity in the form of dozens of empty promises.

Harold looked around the small but neat two-bedroom bungalow he shared with Mercy. They could easily have afforded a larger home, but they had not been blessed with children, so Harold refused to waste money on a larger house, especially as any available space would undoubtedly have been promptly filled by his relatives' offspring. While Harold may not have succeeded in procreating, his twin had more than made up for this. Evans had made a positive contribution to the strengthening of the gene pool in Zambia, by fathering children in all ten provinces.

He was very proud of his home, small as it was. He believed his combination of excellent taste and home improvement skills garnered from running his hardware store had resulted in a veritable delight. The money he saved by not having a large house in Kafue wouldn't be frittered away, either. Harold's plan was to build a mansion on a farm plot when he retired, back in the village his grandfather came from, and to be the talk of that village. Oh how they would admire his mansion! His relatives would stop making snide comments about his Harris Tweed jacket; indeed, they would all want one in order to aspire to be at his level. He could just imagine all his relatives coming to ask his advice. He was busy enjoying this reverie when the rather incongruous vision of Evans wearing a Harris Tweed jacket and parading around his mansion with a cup of tea in hand rather spoiled it and jolted him back to the task at hand.

He was busy at work with a saw in his bedroom, cutting into their king sized bed. This was harder work than he was used to, for his skills leaned towards directing home improvements rather than executing them, but it would be worth it in the end. This, after all, was to protect his health, and Mercy's too, so that they could live out his dream of retiring in style. (Mercy's life was mainly centred around kitchen parties, weddings and church meetings, all of which were usually avoided by Harold, except for those occasions where he decided that the church would benefit from his valuable opinions on some matter or another. Consequently, she wasn't looking forward to his retirement with the same passion as he was, although the idea of sitting on a veranda, admiring an assortment of fruit trees and whiling away the hours chatting to relatives did sound quite appealing).

Earlier on, Harold had started on his project

by spending an hour marking COVID-19 safe social distancing lanes throughout the house, each labelled either Harold or Mercy. It was of course a pure accident that his mother-in-law, a traditionally built woman with a tongue laced with venom and an attitude befitting the villain in a long, drawn-out Nigerian drama, did not have a lane allocated to her. That might mean she had to stay in the garden during her daily visit and that her usual offering of deprecating remarks about Harold had to be conducted in the garden. After all, the pandemic had changed lives everywhere, and Harold didn't see why nagging mothers-in-law couldn't share some of the pain.

His lines were very neat, in-keeping with Harold's personality, and each instance of a *Harold* or *Mercy* marking was perfectly aligned with the others. There could be no doubt over what was what and who was supposed to be where. He was confident that his carefully thought through plan would help keep them safe.

It took another hour of sawing, puffing and resting, but by early evening Harold was able to stand in the middle of the space that had until recently been occupied by their king size bed. He admired his handiwork. The combination of his ingenuity and some tools he had brought home from his hardware store had paid off. He was standing between two separate beds. He took out his measuring tape. Anchoring one end of it under the closest corner of the bed in Mercy's lane, he stretched it out. At eighty centimetres the tape was touching the bed on his half of the room – not nearly far enough apart yet.

Harold was just shoving the beds farther apart when Mercy walked in, with a bewildered look on her face. "What are you doing, dear?"

Harold measured the distance again; the two beds were now a full metre apart. He nodded to himself, satisfied. "We have to be safe, dear." He pointed at the lane markings on the floor. "This is social distancing."

Mercy folded her arms beneath her ample chest and glared at him. "It will be even safer if you sleep on the couch!"

"Yes! Great idea!" Harold brightened visibly, and pulled a blanket off the bed. "Now I just need to be going with my handi santitiza."

4: THIS TIME

Harold's pride and joy, a pale yellow ("pale gold" in Harold speak) old ("vintage") 1980s Mercedes Benz C-Class had been the cause of a bad start to his day. He had to go into "that town" (as he referred to the capital city, Lusaka), but the car had decided that it really didn't feel like going. This did nothing to improve Harold's mood; he had not slept well. While the couch offered good social distancing in comparison to sleeping in the same room as Mercy and breathing in her expelled snores, it had a few lumps that had decided to spend the night reminding him of some of the tenderest parts of his body.

This left Harold with a conundrum. He pulled his smart phone from the pocket of his Harris Tweed jacket and thought. He could call his mechanic, who would take at least an hour to walk the 100 or so metres from his garage to Harold's house, never wore a mask and had declared coronavirus a fiction. He would almost certainly talk at length about the conspiracy to steal all his life savings (which, Harold suspected, didn't actually exist in the first place) after Bill Gates personally injected a microchip into his shoulder while pretending to vaccinate him. Or, he could lower himself to the indignity of catching a minibus into the city, another nemesis.

He opted for the latter in the interests of both time and his general sanity. As he approached the bus stop Harold saw with a heavy heart that he was going to get two nemeses for the price of one; waiting at the pick-up point was his layabout twin.

Evans, on the other hand, brightened considerably as Harold approached. He had been trying to calculate how he would manage to get everything his live-in girlfriend had instructed him to buy in town, then pay for the bus back, and still have enough to share the wealth in Sam's Tavern on the way home. This problem had now solved itself, as Evans knew Harold would rather pay for him than have Evans announce loudly to other passengers that his pillar-of-the-community brother couldn't even afford to help him with the bus fare. It was an approach that had worked so often that Evans didn't even bother mentioning it to Harold, he just needed to say "Bro!" loudly with a massive grin and he could be assured of his fare being paid.

Evans saw minibuses as a national resource. A treasure, if you will. He couldn't understand why people like his twin hated them so much; nor could he understand why certain classes of Zambian society viewed minibus drivers with complete and utter disdain.

Minibus drivers, Evans believed, were the

knights of the road. If you found a traffic jam, a helpful minibus driver or his trusty call-boy would be outside the minibus, risking their lives in the traffic, directing and restoring some sort of order. If a fellow road user had a breakdown, the minibus drivers would lean out of their windows and offer helpful advice and insights, all at no charge. And, if you happened to have had a bad day and be desperately in need of a bit of light libation, they were generally happy to let you have a swig of their own personal stash.

Harold's view could not have been more different. To him, minibus drivers were just a problem, a blight on the landscape of humanity. If you found a traffic jam, you could be sure that one or more overloaded minibuses, loading or unloading passengers with scant consideration for the queue of traffic behind them were slap-bang in the middle of it all. Generally, they would also have call-boys sitting perched on the window, with their trousers half-way down their buttocks. If you were unfortunate enough to have a problem with your car, the drivers would lean out and jeer at you – proffering insults about your ability to purchase a Benz but your inability to service it. (For some reason that Harold couldn't grasp, they always seemed to take issue with his Harris Tweed jacket; he put that down to a complete ignorance of the world of fashion.) If all that wasn't evidence enough of the trouble they could cause, they were nearly always drunk, Harold believed, driving alongside bottles filled with kachasu and other illicit local concoctions.

To Evans, it was more than just the minibus drivers that made the whole experience so valuable. Minibus trips were a source of opportunity – a chance to gain a date from a good-looking woman; a chance to increase his personal wealth through the carelessness of a fellow passenger; a chance to get some gossip or stories that would in turn get a few drinks bought for him at Sam's Tavern. Evans could get a lot out of any minibus journey: he just had to make sure he wore the right political party t-shirt.

Harold stopped at what he judged to be a safe distance from Evans, at least a metre away from him. Actually, Harold thought to himself, a safe distance from Evans would be to be on another continent altogether. That option not being immediately available, a metre apart would have to suffice.

"How is home?" Evans asked. "I should come visit."

"Home is fine," Harold replied. "Don't visit, we are isolating."

"Awe, Bro, me I don't count. Relatives are allowed."

"Even if you santitize for an hour, reeelatives are not arrowed. We are trying to stop convid-19."

"Serious, Bro, it's fine," Evans moved closer to Harold and tried to embrace him, swiping at his jacket and quietly relieving him of his cell phone in the process. "I can even come today!"

Harold backed off from Evans, who now seemed to be fidgeting with a hand behind his back. Writing that off to Evans being Evans, Harold saw with relief that the minibus was approaching, recklessly careering around the corner at breakneck speed, towing an open trailer for luggage.

That morning, the minibus was already overcrowded. The conductor was literally hanging out of the door, jumping off as it screeched to a halt, narrowly missing Harold's toes.

"What's wrong with you?" he asked the conductor, who simply gave a wide, toothy smile. "Where is your mask?"

"It is finished," the conductor answered. "I am getting another one."

"When?" Harold demanded.

"When we reach, boss. Do you see a place this side with masks?" He gestured at their surroundings, which apart from a lone, closed mobile money booth were devoid of activity.

"Tiye, boss, tiye."

Evans pushed past Harold and clambered aboard. "Bro, there's plenty of space," he called out, as he squeezed himself onto a seat designed for two, perching haphazardly in between a frail looking elderly man and a traditionally built woman. The old man coughed violently.

"No way am getting in there", Harold said. "You, boy, can't you make room?"

"Boss, there is plenty space, your friend he has managed, you see?"

"Your bus is full!"

"This bus is never full, bwana. The only thing that gets full this side is yo' pit latrine."

Harold bristled at this, wheezed, and turned to look at the trailer. It was fairly empty this morning. It just held a few parcels, a goat tied to the side with a bit of rope, and a handful of chickens sitting there with their feet tied together. Seeing the goat looking quite happy gave him an idea. Using his measuring tape, he satisfied himself that it was a metre apart from the minibus itself, sanitised the side of the trailer and clambered in. Yes, it was somewhat undignified but significantly safer.

The conductor was not sure what to do about this man in the strange jacket who was insisting on riding in the trailer. In the end, he settled for profit; he told Harold that the trailer was first-class, reserved for those who wanted to ride in isolation and charged him triple.

This didn't sit well with Harold, but the conductor gave him three choices: squeeze in next to the coughing old man; pay triple to ride in the trailer; or walk into town. Harold decided paying up was the least undesirable option.

With the matter settled, the conductor banged on the roof of the minibus and the contraption started off again with a lurch. On that day, Harold became a social media celebrity. He was snapped several times by passing motorists (often while the goat was alternating between its two primary objectives of trying to achieve dominance of the available space and ascertaining whether Harris Tweed jackets were edible); before the minibus even reached Lusaka, he was destined to become the nation's newest meme.

Evans, meanwhile, was having a great time. Because he had boarded at the same time and at the same stop as the pompous man who was insisting in riding in the trailer with the goat and chickens, he was the star storyteller, and managed to land himself several swigs of the driver's stash and a date for the weekend.

Later that day, Harold was back in Kafue when he realised his smart phone was missing. With some irritation, he concluded it must have got lost or been stolen when he was getting on or off the minibus. That was one of the many reasons why he never normally used buses.

For a brief moment he contemplated filing a police report on the loss of his phone, but he remembered just in time that his last run in with the Kafue's finest. At a roadblock, which had seemed rather pointless to him, he had called the Inspector an "incompetent buffoon" and been threatened with a night in the cell for his impudence. Whatever other skills the Inspector might or might not have had, he certainly had a long memory, which was useful for maintaining order in a small town like Kafue, but didn't do much for Harold's chances of being able to file a report on the theft without considerable ridicule, even more paperwork, and, most significantly, being given an extensive run around. Such was the price Harold often had to pay for sharing his insights with those who he judged to have an inferior intellect to his. While there were times when he felt that price was worth it, there were also times when the individual concerned could make Harold's life very difficult indeed, and this was one of those.

And so it was that Harold found himself outside the service centre for his cell phone network provider. Harold braced himself. He rarely left that den of brightly coloured signage, posters filled with over-promises, shining gadgets and queues chaperoned by dawdling customer service staff feeling better than when he went in.

In Harold's experience, a visit to a cell phone network service centre was much like going to a less-than-sanitary hospital. You went in there trying to resolve one problem and came back out with something you really, really didn't want.

The even bigger challenge in the current pandemic, was that now you could get the disease you didn't want from the cell phone network service centre just as easily as you could from the hospital. Possibly with even greater ease, thought Harold, as he watched the guard at the door pull his face mask down to flirt with a passing young lady.

Harold was about to pull open the door, when the guard put out a flabby arm to stop him. "I have my own santitiza", Harold said, taking a guess at what was coming. He waved it at the guard.

"You have to sanitise with this same sanitiser," the guard told him. "Us we don't know what you are putting in there."

Harold relented, and went inside. He was met by a grinning young man, clad in a bright t-shirt proclaiming how wonderful the cell network was. Seeing a branded t-shirt wasn't exactly a shock; the cell phone providers produced so many t-shirts that one only had to walk past a cell phone tower to acquire one. The only people that seemed to outdo the networks on t-shirt give-aways were the political parties, busy shouting "uuuyo" from the back of their trucks as they lobbed t-shirts at unsuspecting passing citizens, each vehicle loaded with enough speakers to flood a stadium with sound, and enough cadres to match. Whether or not you got an extra t-shirt for being in the truck when its side panels collapsed and you fell out, as had happened to an excitable group of cadres a few days earlier, Harold was not sure.

"Please take a ticket, sir." The young man pointed towards a machine.

Harold sighed. These ticket systems never seemed to offer the option he was looking for. He always somehow ended up in the wrong queue, and he had a feeling that today would not be an exception. He scrolled through the choices on the screen, muttering to himself about what a contradiction it was to the big poster above it that advised customers to "Use mobile money, stay contact-less, stay safe." No matter how hard he looked at the choices, he couldn't see one that suited his needs. What on earth was a "new generation SIM upgrade"? What was "comprehensive data assistance"? What was "handset consultation"? Why couldn't it just say things like "Buy a new phone because some crook has stolen your existing one"?

By this time, there were a few people waiting behind Harold, and the young man felt the need to hurry him up. "Sir", he urged him, "you are delaying other customers."

"I can't understand your system! Tell me which to pick, my phone was stolen" Harold said.

"Just pick any. No specialists are working today because of COVID-19, so any option will work the same."

Harold almost exploded, before remembering the he really needed a phone, so getting forcibly removed from the store would not be a great idea. He sighed, muttered some unintelligible insult about the origins of the young man rendering him incapable of producing offspring, punched a random option on the screen and took a ticket. He knew full well that this meant he would end up in the slowest-moving queue; it was always the way in cell phone stores.

The one saving grace, Harold thought to himself, was that everyone in the store was masked up, there were Perspex shields in front of the counter staff, and the queues appeared to be sticking to the social distancing marks on the floor.

Fifteen minutes later, Harold was getting restless. The line he had joined had moved at first, but now there was an elderly man at the front of the queue, who had clearly done no thinking whatsoever while standing in the queue. Such people drove Harold nuts. It was worse in the fast-food outlets; people would queue for ten minutes staring up at the menu, get to the front of the queue, then, when they reached the cashier, ask him or her what the options were. Then they would not get to the point of making up their mind until the cashier had gone through the entire menu twice.

The elderly man clearly didn't understand the reason for the Perspex shield, and seemed convinced that the young lady behind the counter couldn't hear him. He pulled down his mask and put his face against the gap between her Perspex shield and the counter, "am asking why my phone balance is saying no minutes when I haven't been calling" he bellowed. It took quite a bit of explaining before the old man could get the hang of having purchased a bundle of things he didn't want that all expired by the time he decided he actually wanted to use them. Harold could relate to that. What on earth would that old man do with an add-on that allowed him to have his text messages played out to him in a cartoon voice, or daily text messages of so-called inspiration from the nation's snobbiest diva?

The old man was finally pacified, and he

moved away from the counter. Harold almost smiled at the sales assistant for having braved him. He even felt sorry for her – until she said to him, "sorry, it's my break, please join that other queue" and walked off before Harold could even recover from the shock.

◆ ◆ ◆

That evening, back in Kafue after an eventful day in Lusaka, Evans decided that making good on his threat to visit Harold at home was simply asking for more long-winded lectures. With his live-in girlfriend expecting some benefit from his visit to the city, Evans did what he did whenever he felt like avoiding conflict – he went to the bar.

Actually, it's not fair to imply that Evans chose to support his favourite bars merely as a form of escape. From his standpoint, if he and his cronies didn't frequent the bar every night, they would be directly responsible for a fall in the nation's GDP. And, in the midst of the election campaigns, surrounded by politicians waffling on about responsible stewardship of the nation's resources, Evans felt compelled to do his bit to sustain the economy.

Sam's Tavern never really changed much. Every few years Sam would feel an urge, get out the same shade of cream paint, and splash it around a bit, irrespective of whether or not he covered some of the regulars in paint splatters at the same time.

Sam took a similar approach to his personal

appearance. Every few years he would get a few new shirts, and that would be that for a while. He always sat in the same spot behind the bar, his enormous bulk perched on a stool designed for someone significantly smaller than him. His stool was in turn perched on a pair of concrete blocks, a deliberate move that made sure he could always look down on those around him. His throne (as he liked to think of it), from which he pronounced judgement on the dilemmas his regulars placed before him, was positioned directly beneath the obligatory framed photo of His Excellency the President. Sam felt that sitting beneath that most prestigious of photographs gave his opinions a certain degree of respectability, as if they were backed by presidential decree. As he was twice as wide as he was tall, if it had been a requirement for Sam's photo to hang alongside the President's, his photo would have had to be landscape format.

Evans was perched opposite Sam, with a woman on either side of him, both of whom he was trying to impress. They had been sitting next to each other when he arrived, and with his usual winning charm, round of compliments, and, more significantly, a round of drinks, he had managed to squeeze himself between them. He was now busy contemplating his prospects, his live-in girlfriend having temporarily been relegated to somewhere at the back of his mind.

That evening, Sam was holding forth at great length on his views about ladies' slippers. In his view, the state of the slippers worn by a woman wore was a firm indicator of how she might treat her man. (The possibility that it might also reflect how the woman's man was treating her was sadly completely lost on him). In Sam's view, a woman who wore worn out slippers around the house but neat and tidy slippers out and about, was a woman who respected her husband and looked after the home. A woman who wore a different pair of glamorous, sparkling or ostentatious slippers almost every day was, he argued, guaranteed only to be after a man's money.

At this point, Evans leant back from his perch and took a surreptitious look at the feet of the woman on either side of him. To the left, slender feet with bright pink toenails sitting in bright pink slippers with an imitation ribbon mounted on them. To the right, slippers with a magenta strap patterned with stars, hosting a pair of large feet on the end of chubby legs with the toenails painted bright orange. This colour combination may have briefly waged war in Evans eyes, but for once he decided that it was not something to comment on. Instead, he concluded that if his evening in the company of these two was to stand any chance of getting interesting, he had better try and dampen down Sam's rant. "As for me, I think that if a woman changes her slippers often she is showing that her man is generous and fashionable," he announced.

"You are wrong," Sam said, firmly. "A woman who is always changing awe is just wanting money all the time. Mo especially if she is painting her toenails too much and putting tuma jewels jewels everywhere. If God had wanted us to have things stuck on nails he would have put them there oready."

Evans took another surreptitious glance downwards to double check that both women had decorations on their toenails. "I think decorated nails are very much in fashion. Me, I like it" Evans beamed at his neighbours. "It is in fashionable in Dubai. Everywhere you go that side, you find women with decorated toenails."

Sam rolled his eyes. "What you know about Dubai, Evans? Kulibe. You haven't even been to Sowse Africa."

"South" Evans told him. "Us who go there all the time we just call it down South. We don't even need to say the Africa because we are going there so many times."

This elicited a snort from Sam and a question from one of the women. "You travel to South Africa?"

"Yes, all the time", Evans bragged. "Ine I was supposed to be there last week; but this coronavirus cancelled it." He paused and turned to face her; she had a huge smile on her face. "There are even whole shops bigger than the mall with only slippers inside, nothing else."

"Ha!" this from Sam. "So that's where you go when you sleep, you go to buy some slippers in Sowse Africa."

"You, you wouldn't know a good slipper if yo'

wife beat you with it!" Evans retorted.

Sam stood up, causing Evans to realise that he had perhaps crossed a line that might jeopardise the status of his never-ending tab. "Women who change slippers all the time are a big plobrem!" he roared.

"Ah, you are right, Sam, always. You are truly a wise man. That is why I come here all the time," he explained to the women beside him.

"So, if you are going to South, will you visit the slippers store?" the woman on his left asked.

"Too much" Evans replied. "Now the pressure, this COVID means I cannot travel."

"Slippers are a waste of money" Sam muttered.

"No, no," the chubby woman objected. "They are fashion and a good price."

"Too true" Evans chorused, and added, before he could stop himself, "I can even buy you some."

"Even me, I am asking for some slippers" added the woman on the right.

Evans turned and beamed at her, eager to impress. This was going to be an interesting night. "Yes, even you."

She stretched her hand towards him. "Give us kabili we go and buy."

As usual, Evans's speeches were fuller than his wallet, so in the end the two had to make do with extracting assurances that purchasing slippers for them was the first thing on his agenda for the next morning.

Evans looked around for a diversion from the

topic of slippers. The TV in the corner was – as ever – on and droning on. This time it was in the middle of a "mask up and stay safe" public service announcement. Evans held up his bottle of beer in front of his face and admired it. "This is how I am staying safe!"

A snort escaped from Sam's girth on his higher perch. "You should be using sanitiser."

"Didn't you listen to the news?" Evans retorted. "Ati alcohol kills the COVID-19."

"Ayi!" Sam's mirth was evident.

"Am serious. They said!"

"You also. It's not the alcohol for drinking."

"I swear, that is the only kind of alcohol am caring about."

"That beer isn't strong enough," Sam grinned enthusiastically. Always able to spot the chance to add a few more Kwacha to Evans's perpetual tab, Sam heaved a large container advertising cooking oil that now contained a clear liquid that could have been anything from undiluted vodka to diluted kerosene onto the bar. "You need spirit, my friend. This can kill anything. Germs, COVID, liver, brains – amapha chilichonse."

Evans climbed onto his bar stool and toasted the bar, grinning away at his audience. "Yes! Give me. Ine I want to live!"

Evans was never quite able to satisfactorily explain to his live-in girlfriend where all the money from the previous day's trip to the bank to collect the money transfer from his latest scheme had gone, why his underwear was on back-to-front, or indeed why that was the only item of clothing he was wearing when he finally got home that night.

5: THAT TIME

The mall was a relatively recent addition to life in Kafue. As the rapidly expanding capital city Lusaka seemed to have more malls than it quite knew what to do with, Evans was quite pleased that he could now save himself more drinking time by not having to take a bus to the city whenever his live-in girlfriend demanded things from him. The argument that the bus fare to Lusaka was more than a loaf of bread and some essential groceries was a very reasonable observation, one that even the crankiest of girlfriends could relate to. The fact that the bus fare also happened to be more than the price of a couple of beers was not lost on Evans, although this wasn't information he generally shared.

He swaggered into the car park and towards the mall, ignoring the sanitation signs instructing him to wash his hands and sanitise thoroughly.

"You! You have to sanitise!" a skinny security guard suddenly called out, from his lackadaisical post leaning against a wall.

"From where?" Evans tried to look innocent – an expression he had developed through all his late home-comings over the years.

"I show you. This side, sah!" He walked across the car park towards the hand-wash bucket, picking his nose with one hand and scratching his butt with the other. Pointing at the hand wash station, he turned to Evans. "It is too much important to be keeping clean, sah, there is some colona viluses."

Evans nodded, making a production of washing his hands. He saw it as a waste of time but given that he had time to waste while waiting for his mates Mulenga and Bwalya to arrive, it wasn't a big deal. He decided to waste more time by getting into a debate with the security guard.

"Me I was told that this virus is only for muzungus; us we can't get it", he told the guard.

"Awe, ah ah. Even my aunty she got it, she is sick in hospital."

"Ohhhhh? Serious?" Evans may have been generally callous about life, but making light of a sick aunty was something one simply didn't do. This also put paid to his plan of killing time by arguing with the security guard, so he opted for a simple muttered "Sorry, mwandi, she will be fine," and wandered off to wait.

Harold, who was properly masked, and carrying his measuring tape and hand sanitiser, reached the mall just in time to witness Evans greeting his mates.

Evans, Mulenga and Bwalya, who was wearing a mask on top of his forehead, met and high-fived each other, arms outstretched.

Harold couldn't quite believe his eyes. The sight of Evans and his cronies slapping each other was just too much for his sensibilities. He stormed over to the trio, waving his measuring tape, pulling down his triple layer of face masks to yell at them. "You! This is not safe! That is not one metre!" he lectured them.

"Yes, it is", Mulenga answered.

"No, that is not arrowed."

"I can show you!" said Mulenga, defiantly. "Me am taller than one metre." He lay on the ground and, in doing so, proved to an increasingly infuriated Harold that he and Evans were in fact more than a metre apart. "See. I tol' you! More than one metre!"

"But you, you, you were trying to high five", spluttered Harold. "You need to distance, santitize and mask up!"

Bwalya pointed enthusiastically at his masked forehead.

"Chill, mudala, am masking!"

"It needs to cover your mouth!" Harold snarled.

"Like yours is, bro!" Evans laughed, causing Harold to scowl and pull his masks back up over his mouth.

"What's wrong with you, you want to die?" At least, that's what Harold was trying to say, but the triple layer of face masks served to muffle his rant.

"Ati what?" Bwalya asked him, his round face frowning hard in mock concentration.

"We can't get you", added Evans, poking his ear with his finger.

Harold growled and pulled his face masks down. "I said, what's wrong with you, you want to die?"

"Dude your mask is down, you are not safe!" Bwalya giggled.

Harold scowled, muttering as he put his masks back up and stomped off in a thoroughly bad mood. He stopped, turned, and waved his hand sanitiser like a weapon. "Santitize or die!" he shouted. Harold turned his back on Evans and his friends and stomped off, leaving them laughing.

Harold was still wound up by his interaction with Evans when he reached the entrance to the main supermarket in the mall. Supermarkets' approach to protecting staff and customers from the pandemic varied wildly. While some chains really didn't care how sick you were, as long as you parted with your cash at some point, others treated shoppers as if they were a biological warfare weapon, ready to disperse germ warfare around their zealously guarded retail territory. In their view, any one shopper could easily be an infected citizen sent by a rival supermarket chain to take out all their staff with a single well-placed sneeze.

The supermarket Harold was about to enter was of the latter variety. As he approached the entrance, three security guards bore down on him from three different directions: one armed with a thermometer; the second with a hand sanitiser spray; and the third with trolley wipes. He felt cornered, and it didn't sit well with him. Moreover, he was – in his view – at least twice as sanitary as any of the guards approaching him. The guard with the thermometer waved it in his general direction and grinned, while the guard with the wipes took the shopping basket from his hand and gave it a vague wipe. Whereas those two performed their duties in a perfunctory, ambivalent fashion, the guard in charge of the hand sanitiser spray clearly loved his job. "Morning bosses" he greeted Harold with a humongous grin. "Welcome, welcome. I just have to sanitise yo' hands."

Harold grimaced at the beaming guard and reluctantly stretched out his palms. The guard sprayed a large enthusiastic dose of hand sanitiser in Harold's general direction, mostly missing his hands but ensuring that any virus on his precious Harris Tweed jacket was certainly done for. "My jacket!" Harold almost squealed the words.

"Sorry bosses, you moved, ine I missed", the guard beamed before putting all his muscle into another massive squirt from the dispenser. This time it hit its mark, with such a dose of liquid that it was literally dripping off Harold's hands.

Harold looked down at the gunk covering his hands. "Am I bathing or what?" he demanded. "This is enough to santitize an army! What am I supposed to do with it?"

"Sorry, sorry, sorry", said the guard, A more accurate verbalisation of his actual attitude would clearly have been "you're supposed to rinse out your big mouth with it."

Evans and his friends watched this altercation with much amusement. Although they were all ready for a beer and a sit down, they had decided that it wouldn't be a good idea to become dehydrated on the walk to Sam's Tavern, and therefore the safest way to avoid this plight was to quench their thirst by buying a beer from the supermarket first. They lined up by the entrance in a docile fashion, palms out for the security guard, as if they were a trio of kids waiting for sweets to be handed out in return for their exemplary behaviour – an experience, one suspects, that Evans and friends had never actually encountered.

Harold glared once more at the guard for good measure. A trip to the supermarket had always been one of Harold's least favourite activities. It generally wreaked havoc with his sense of order, especially given that this particular supermarket appeared to be rearranged about once every two weeks, presumably with the dual aim of befuddling shoppers into buying more while making sure that the staff had something to do. If it were not for rearranging the place frequently, the store would probably have needed about 20 less of the manager's relatives in its employ. Needless to say, at least half of those relatives didn't know the whereabouts of any particular product, nor did they have the slightest clue as to what they were actually doing.

Ever since the onset of the COVID-19

pandemic, the ineptitude of the supermarket staff had taken on a whole extra dimension in the form of their general inability to wear a face mask correctly. Yes, it was true that they were all wearing a mask, but the matter of how to wear it was clearly not governed by any form of in-store consensus.

Take the stock handler, Michael, for instance. He knew exactly how to wear his face mask. It was supposed to make sure he could breathe nicely, so he always was very careful to sit it just below his nostrils.

For the chatterboxes, like old Mr Banda who was in charge of weighing vegetables while rabbiting on to his surrounding colleagues (or anyone who would listen, for that matter) about something completely irrelevant, there was really only one way to wear their face masks: proudly wrapped around their chin, below their perpetually open mouths.

Then there were the fashionistas who lurked among the supermarket staff. Like Precious, who clearly felt that the best place for her face mask was dangling over her ear like an extra earring, complementing the large nickel plated hoops that were already hanging there. That look worked well for Brian, too, although he tended to forgo the giant hooped earrings. For Chika, the face mask was the perfect adornment to her heavily bleached wrist; her hands were so well-tended and nails so manicured that, for her, placing any product on a shelf was an exercise to be avoided at all costs. And there was no way she was using a face mask to hide that stunning lippy her latest boyfriend had bought for her.

Daisy, who sat heavily on a wobbly swivel chair behind the cigarette counter all day, swaying from left to right (and bobbling up and down as the swivel chair squeaked under her ample behind), was proud that she'd earned the right to have a full Perspex face-shield from her boss. She had a chronic cough already, one that she chewed raw garlic and ginger several times a day for. It was quite a fight to get permission to wear the full face shield, but the double-pronged attack of her condition and her being the boss' wife's kid sister had helped seal the deal. So she wore it with pride, the shield set at an angle that pretty much made sure that everyone who came within three metres of her was guaranteed to get a good strong helping of her garlicky breath.

Still, Harold noted, despite all those permutations, at least none of them was wearing their mask on their forehead in the style set by Evans's idiotic friend. No matter which way he looked at it, this pandemic was not making the traumatic experience of grocery shopping any less stressful.

The arrangement of products was filled with anachronisms that waged war on Harold's ordered view of life. Why, for instance, were toothpicks shelved in the same aisle as engine oil? And was that the reason why so many minibus drivers chewed on toothpicks while hanging out their windows and contributing to the commotion on the roads?

These were just a few of the thoughts that troubled Harold as he made his way around the supermarket, with the added headache of being all too aware that the chances of another run in with Evans and his fellow layabouts were very high indeed.

Harold had made it safely all the way round the supermarket, and even managed not to scream at Precious and her dangling mask as she casually sat on the cases of soft drinks that until that very moment he had been contemplating purchasing. No matter how exciting the cola advert he had seen was, the image of Precious plonking herself heavily down on top of something that could have gone near his mouth was something that would give him terrors for weeks to come. He found a queue that looked like it might move at least slightly faster than a three-legged tortoise and joined it.

Unfortunately for Harold, Evans and his friends had just picked their beers off the shelves, opened them, and while trying to avoid sloshing too much on to their political party regalia (after all, they needed to look respectable in case they got an opportunity to join a rally and get some free lunch later in the day), they too saw the queue Harold was in as too good an opportunity to miss. After all, there were a good number of things to do in Kafue, mostly involving the consumption of beer, but winding up Harold was without a doubt among the most entertaining of their pastimes.

Evans put his finger to his lips in a shushing motion to his friends, and the trio crept up behind Harold, ignoring the social distancing markers on the floor.

Harold turned around sharply, but just as he did so Evans took a large step backwards to the mark on the floor, followed swiftly by Bwalya and Mulenga. Harold glared at Evans, suspecting that there was mischief afoot, and faced the front again. The moment Harold looked away, Evans, Bwalya, Mulenga shuffled forward. Harold started to turn, and the three stepped back to the correct markers again.

Harold glared at them and the trio all put their very best "who, me?" expressions on in a pathetic attempt to look innocent. In unison they waved their beer bottles at Harold and toasted him, shouting "Santitiza!"

Harold snorted and turned to face the front again.

Evans, Bwalya, Mulenga shuffled forward again. Harold spun around quickly, and the three leapt back to the correct markers.

"Keep your distance!" This was muffled by his three masks, as Harold waved his first at them.

"We are", Evans and Bwalya chorused together.

Mulenga leaned over and tapped Bwalya on his shoulder. "What's wrong with this dude?"

"Stop touching each other!" Harold said. He

leaned to one side to look past Evans and Bwalya and addressed Mulenga. "You should santitize now!"

Harold turned back around and resumed his position in the queue. Evans, Bwalya, Mulenga shuffled forward again; this time Harold caught them at it.

"I see you!" came his muffled triumphant bellow. "You are trying to infect me!" Harold shoved Evans backwards. He staggered and fell into Bwalya and Mulenga, who in turn stumbled, turning the whole queue into something of a slapstick farce.

"You touched me!" Evans shouted. He turned to play to the rest of the customers in the queue, who were now paying close attention to the drama. "He touched me! He is not" – he paused to use his fingers as quote marks, mimicking Harold – "social distancing!"

Harold was stunned, and the astonishment showed on his round face. He was confounded. What on earth was going on?

"You've seen, pipo!" Evans continued his performance. "This man doesn't know the rules!"

"Too bad, too bad-." This was from Bwalya, sucking his teeth noisily.

"Ala! Some pipo don't care!" Mulenga chipped in. The three friends were enjoying the crowd's attention, knowing full well this would now be a story in a good number of Kafue homes for the rest of the day.

For Harold, this was just too much. He threw his shopping basket to the floor and stormed off, literally stamping his feet as he went, leaving Evans, Bwalya, Mulenga and their captive audience laughing at his tantrum.

◆ ◆ ◆

It took Harold some time to cool down from the indignity of the incident in the supermarket. Once his breathing had returned to normal, he decided that he needed to protect his territory from his unsanitary brother and his threat of a visit. He had seen on TV that in some other countries people were not allowed to visit other's homes during peak coronavirus waves, and this seemed like an excellent idea to him. If he had his way, the concept of barring home visits to certain individuals – Evans, for instance – would be extended indefinitely. However, with election campaigns in the country in full force, there was no way the president would enforce such a policy. At least, he wouldn't unless he could think of a good reason to exclude his door-to-door campaigners from compliance, other than their usual complete disregard for the law and general societal etiquette.

If Harold were president, there would be an end to such nonsense. Evans and his fellow layabout cronies would have to do a decent day's work and contribute positively to society for a change. The economy would grow, and, moreover, he would be loved and respected for the wise man he was. He could well remember being asked to describe himself in a team-building exercise some months back, and he had proudly announced to his team members: "I am an interrectual." There had been much applause and laughter; he had clearly understood how adored he was.

Harold had several run-ins with political party cadres, and none of them had left him anything less than exasperated. They drove down the wrong side of the road, honking their minibus' horns as if they were driving a dying patient somewhere, rather than merely trying to save someone in the death throes of a political career. They were rude to you, and if you met them on the street or in a store, they would usually harass you unless you promised them on your father's life that you would vote for their candidate. Harold always caved in and promised, although he always kept his fingers crossed behind his back as he took pride in the fact that he was not a liar.

It had occurred to Harold more than once that his brother's less than exemplary behaviour was probably a direct result of the time he spent with such people, but there was literally no getting through to him. Or them, for that matter. The last time the cadres had made a door-to-door visit at Harold's house, he had ended up so wound up arguing with them about corruption and being astounded by how little they knew compared to him, that he had ended up having an asthma attack. He had come to the conclusion as he lay down recovering after their visit, that politicians could be credited with putting the ass into asthma.

With all these thoughts running through his head, Harold decided it was time for some affirmative action. If his home and garden was a contaminated zone, Evans could not be reasonably allowed in. Armed with a measuring tape and some rope, Harold made his way outside. Stepping through his gate, he smiled in satisfaction. Each time he viewed his iron gate from the roadside, with the neatly manicured grass that ran along the side of his railing fence, he was proud. It had taken him many hours of berating his somewhat disinterested gardener (who, infuriatingly was Mercy's Aunt's husband and therefore could not be sacked or disciplined), but Harold had finally won his battle and had a perimeter he could be proud of. Living in a suburb like this meant that certain standards were expected of you, and Harold took great effort to not only live up to those standards, but also – at least from his perspective – to reach greater heights. Local opinion on the appearance of his surroundings was firmly divided: on the one hand, you had Harold, who considered himself stylish and a thought-leader, and then on the other hand, you had everybody else.

Harold's home was in one of the more upmarket areas of town, where those who were fortunate enough to be on the higher end of the income scale lived. It was a ma yardi suburb, where each house had its own private, usually walled, garden. The cars were Mercedes Benz (like his vintage pride and joy), BMWs or good quality SUVs and 4x4s. The yards were – generally – well maintained, and one didn't usually have to worry about water supply and keeping one's fruit trees healthy. Indeed, Harold's biggest worry as far as his avocado, guava and mango trees went was making sure that their gardener wasn't pilfering the majority of the fruits and sharing them with anyone who happened to admire Harold's trees and knock on the gate. The gardener didn't see it Harold's way. He felt that fruits were shared property, available to each and every person, the way God intended it.

Harold surveyed his street with pride. In the high density housing areas, the compounds, like the one where his twin lived, the streets weren't lined with security fences harbouring immaculately trimmed gardens patrolled by slightly less immaculate security guards. Evans's suburb didn't really have streets, per se; they were more like interconnecting dirt tracks, barely wide enough to accommodate a vehicle as it squeezed past row after row of tiny homes, avoiding children darting out from every angle possible. Those homes didn't have gardens, and most didn't have power or running water. And when rainy season came with a vengeance, the roads in Evans's suburb became mini-streams, with portions alternating between large static pools that were home to clouds of mosquitoes and lumpy bits of rock that were destined to attack the undercarriage of one's vehicle. Harold, on the other hand, never had to worry about such things, for the street he lived on was nicely tarred, lined with jacaranda trees, and with storm drains on either side, ready to carry the rainwater away to some less fortunate part of town.

Harold fished his measuring tape from his pocket and began the complicated process of ensuring a one metre safety zone. He whistled as he worked, for he was in his element. He knew he was right, and that everybody else would realise this sooner or later. He was also well aware that an additional benefit of living in a more upmarket suburb was that the roads were generally quiet, which meant there were no witnesses to his display of technical precision; his concentration would not be interrupted by some enthusiastic spectator full of unhelpful but well-meaning advice.

Having worked out distances, Harold took some rope and wound it around the jacaranda trees that lined the road, creating an additional boundary a very exact one metre away from his fence. He stood back and admired his labours; it was time for the final touch. He got some sheets of paper and wrote "COVID-19 Isolation Zone Keep Clear" on them. That should be enough to keep Evans out of his home. Harold would have been very happy if it were also enough to keep Mercy's nagging mother away, but he doubted it would be. He clearly remembered the time she had crossed in front of an Independence Day military parade of tanks and armoured vehicles just so that she could tell him off for having forgotten to buy his wife a new chitenge for the celebrations.

Having come home to the roasting of his life on the night when he arrived home in just his underwear, Evans had decided that there would be decidedly less listening to do if he got home earlier than usual; so it was that he found himself whiling away the late afternoon sun sitting outside his house, swigging beer that he'd bought take-away on his tab at Sam's. This was one of his favourite spots, when he wasn't getting roasted, for he could sit there within a literal spitting distance of the roadside, watching all who passed. His road was at the edge of the high-density housing area, which meant that anyone in that part of Kafue could be seen coming and going, putting Evans first in line for some of the gossip, and, consequently, making him wealthier in his own way. After all, gossip could be traded for a snack or a drink. He leaned back in the ragged armchair he dragged outside for occasions such as this, where he could sit with his feet up on an upturned empty beer crate and watch people saunter, shuffle, stroll, waddle or hurry past the dilapidated road sign just beyond the left wall of his house. It marked the town boundary between Kafue on Evans's side and Chilanga on the other, proudly announcing *You are now leaving Kafue, drive safely* on the side Evans could see, and *Welcome to Kafue* on the side he couldn't. Why people should only drive safely once they had left the town, he had never quite figured out, despite spending many an afternoon sitting in the setting sun, watching people drive recklessly past the sign in either direction.

He was quite comfortable in his site and service home in Kafue, a small square home with one bedroom, a small kitchen space and a living room, decorated inside and out with a recent lick of sandstone paint (thanks to a pretty clerk at Harold's hardware store, and, of course, to Harold, although as usual he was unaware of this). Evans was one of the luckier ones in the area he lived in – he had electricity, the latrine was only used by him and his live-in girlfriend and one other family, and he had a water point just around the corner, which meant the trek for water was short. The rent was cheap, the landlord lived far away and, in an unusual twist of fate for that part of the world, didn't have any relatives nearby who he could call on to harass Evans when the rent was late. And, for some inexplicable reason, it always was. The reason probably would have been clearer had Evans asked Sam, but asking Sam's opinion was never very high on Evans's list of priorities. Moreover, perhaps understandably, Sam was not in a rush to enlighten Evans as to where the bulk of his money went.

That afternoon Evans was feeling quite pleased with himself. He had managed to pacify his live-in girlfriend with the groceries he had bought at the mall, and while at it he had once again managed to postpone any talk of a wedding, this time by explaining that he was doing his civic duty by helping to stop the spread of coronavirus and couldn't possibly condone planning a ceremony at this point in time. He had standards, and a would-be wife should of course respect that, or else she wouldn't be much of a wife. (Evans did indeed have high standards – mostly centred on his core principle of not using the same excuse more than once a month).

Having settled that matter on a higher moral plane, he was also able to extricate himself from any household duties by using the excuse that he intended to dutifully tackle them "mailo". (He had every intention, whenever "mailo" happened to come around, of having an urgent appointment somewhere else – anywhere else, but most likely involving a meeting at Sam's Tavern rather than somewhere else.) These carefully constructed arguments, combined with the occasional winning grin, had left Evans free to spend the evening doing what he did best.

He sat there, doing nothing, occasionally fidgeting with his smart phone – a relatively recent acquisition, an unwitting gift from his twin. Evans's live-in girlfriend was surprised by how many household appliances Harold had given his brother. Harold would have been just as surprised to discover how generous he had been. In Evans's view, to take from one's twin was not stealing, it was simply reallocation of mutual property into the correct hands.

He was absently-mindedly scrolling through Twitter when one tweet caught his attention.

Lockdown from tomorrow: Lusaka, Kafue, Mazabuka! Chilanga exempted.

This, for Evans, was not good news at all. Lockdown would mean no leaving the house, no way of escaping demands from his woman, no opportunity for shirking. A whole horde of "seeing as you are home you should..." tasks flew through his mind – in fact, all the tasks he had managed to avoid this afternoon through his carefully constructed arguments, plus a few more thrown in for good measure. And the prospect terrified him.

He put down his beer and scratched his head. He looked out at his surroundings, surveying them once again, and this time he looked a little harder at the road sign. As he stared past the edge of the yard at the fading *You are now leaving Kafue, drive safely* sign on the roadside, a moment of inspiration struck him.

6: LELO (TODAY)

Evans was fast asleep when the first light touched Kafue the next morning. His live-in girlfriend, who generally got up with the chickens, gave his body a contemptuous kick and got on with her morning. He snorted loudly and turned in his sleep, splatters of red paint, dirt and grime all over him. She had been fast asleep when he came to bed, and she had decided that whatever the story behind his appearance was, it could probably wait.

She went outside to start the charcoal brazier and stopped in irritation. The surroundings, which she distinctly recalled leaving cleanly swept, were now a mess of heaps of dirt, stones and other rubble. The *You are now leaving Kafue, drive safely* sign was very definitely not where it usually was. Someone – and she had a very clear idea of who – had moved the sign to the right hand side of the house, beyond the edge of their site.

She turned to go back inside, ready to drag Evans out of bed and give him a much needed roasting, and her jaw dropped. Where last night had been a clean, whitewashed wall, today there was a dirty, not quite so white wall with *Chilanga Mansion* painted on it in big red letters.

With a deep breath and a very loud grunt, Evans's live-in girlfriend picked up a shovel that he had left lying by the door step, and stepped back into the house, wielding it.

◆ ◆ ◆

Evans had developed several large bruises by the time he ran into Harold later that day. During the rather extensive lecturing it had become clear to Evans that his girlfriend really didn't understand that he had saved her from being restricted by the lock-down, and that he was acting out of the goodness of his heart. She didn't understand that by moving the house across the civic boundary into Chilanga they would no longer be forced to stay at home for days on end. By Evans's logic, they were now from Chilanga, and that meant that they could visit whatever establishments they felt like visiting. However, his selfless act of spending the whole night doing some heavy labour in order to save the house from being in a lockdown zone had gone unrewarded. Worse than that, he had been deprived of any form of breakfast and told in no uncertain terms to go and be selfless somewhere else.

Ever resourceful, Evans had managed to pilfer a fruit-hook, and, while strolling along had managed to help himself to the fruits of his neighbours' labour. Evans decided that he would head towards the ma yardi area of town where his brother lived, as it was likely his new hook would reap more profitable fruits there. Sometimes when fishing for fruit one would accidentally hook a hose-pipe or some other garden implement of value. Most ma yardi homes had fierce dogs and the owners mostly wanted passers-by to let sleeping dogs lie, and he was happy to oblige them. So, if he was stuck with a garden implement that had accidentally got stuck to his hook, it wasn't his fault, and it was better that he should profit economically from the mishap rather than carry some pointless item around all day.

In the back of his mind, Evans was also hopeful that he might manage to chance upon some late breakfast at his twin's home. While Harold was about as welcoming as the dogs in the area, Mercy was always happy to feed Evans. In her view, relatives were important, even her husband's relatives, and she was of the opinion that Evans was far too skinny. His live-in girlfriend didn't know how a man should be fed, she believed. However, she had long since tired of trying to find a more suitable match for Evans. With the thought of breakfast firmly entrenched in his mind, Evans turned into the tree-lined street where Harold lived.

At roughly the same time, Harold had decided to leave his COVID-19 free zone and safety perimeter to go and check up on his store. He didn't really trust Mercy's young brothers who ran the store when he wasn't around. His biggest concern was this: the store was supposed to be closed, because Kafue was in lock-down, and he knew that if he checked the books the revenue for the day would be zero. That was exactly what had been the case during the last lockdown. Oddly enough, after the last lockdown, when the store re-opened, the stock seemed to be less than it should have been, and Harold had developed a sneaking suspicion that perhaps his in-laws had opened the store on those days when he was keeping safe from COVID-19 by relaxing in his favourite arm-chair at home, and had been selling goods off the record and making some money at his expense.

Harold turned a corner and saw Evans a short distance in ahead of him. He took a moment to pray that Evans would not recognise him behind his layer of masks, looked around for hiding places, and for a moment contemplated getting into the drainage ditch that ran alongside the road. However, a quick reflection on the sort of things he'd seen float in that ditch put paid to that idea.

Sighing heavily, Harold eyed the mask-free Evans suspiciously as he approached him. The bruises looked like they had a long story attached, and the presence of the fruit-hook just served to emphasise this. Harold decided not to ask, opting instead for their usual perfunctory greetings.

Evans did an about turn and started to walk alongside his brother. Harold stepped to one side, reminding his twin to keep a safe one-metre distance, especially as he wasn't wearing a mask. Evans assured him that he took coronavirus very seriously, so much so that he felt it his responsibility to spend the day with his twin, protecting him from potential sources of the virus. As he explained this, he veered ever nearer Harold, who in turn veered further and further into the road, trying hard to keep the correct distance between them.

"I am going to check on the store, I have to be sure it is in lockdown" Harold informed his brother. "It will be hard work, I might have to move a lot of things," he added brightly, hoping that the words "hard work" would dissuade Evans from joining him. However, Evans was never easily dissuaded once he had decided something was a good idea, and on this occasion his good idea was that perhaps there might be some items in Harold's shop that didn't tally up nicely on the balance sheet, and thus Evans could be useful to his brother by finding them a proper home elsewhere.

"In these times, bro, we need to stick together. We are family!" a beaming Evans pronounced. "It's just how Grandfather would want us to be."

At the mention of their grandfather, Harold knew he had lost the argument. Grandfather's wishes were something he could not go against. If it hadn't been for their late grandfather's support, wisdom and benevolence, he would not be the pillar of Kafue society he was today. He would have to find another way to lose Evans, preferably before his roving eye had a chance to admire Harold's stock.

Harold was preoccupied trying to think of a suitable ruse as they strolled along, so much so that they had been walking for almost five minutes before he realised that Evans had reduced the one metre safe separation until they were walking shoulder to shoulder. He stepped abruptly away from his twin as they reached a street vendor selling grilled maize on a charcoal brazier. The woman was dusty, and her face-mask was lying on the ground. She picked it up as they drew near but didn't actually get round to putting it on.

Evans rubbed his hands. "OK, OK, maize... it's been long!"

"I'm hungry" Harold admitted, "but there is no way I can go near that woman. She is not safe!"

"You can't" Evans laughed, "Ine, I can." He handed the pole to a horrified Harold and swaggered towards the seller.

Harold popped open his ever-present hand-sanitiser and liberally sanitised the wooden pole of the fruit-hook – and not just because of his extreme scepticism about Evans's hygiene levels. He wouldn't put it past Evans to have stolen it from a pile of items waiting to be disinfected.

"This brother of mine ala..." Harold muttered to himself. As he finished sanitising the pole, an idea popped into his head. "Mama!" He called out to the seller. "How much is one maize?"

Harold lifted the pole and waved it in the direction of the brazier. With much puffing and panting behind his mask, and a close call with the maize vendor's left ear, he managed to hook a maize cob, and pulled down his mask to take a bite, before immediately putting it back into place.

The maize seller closed her open mouth, glared, and opened her mouth again. "Eh-eh!" she said, after a pause. "Ati bwanji, mudala?"

"Don't worry, ama paying you." Harold fished around in his trouser pocket for a note and was reaching towards the woman with it when he recoiled in fear. This looked to be far too much of a risk and would breach the one metre safe distance. One could never be too careful. He flattened the note and sprayed it with sanitiser. "Am keeping you safe", he announced, proudly.

"Passeni ndalama, mudala!"

"Now now, it's coming." He folded the note in half, and again, and again, until it was a small enough wedge to throw.

The seller picked up the note, and unfolded it, before tucking it away somewhere inside her bra. "Do you want change?" she asked Harold, enjoying the disgust apparent on his face.

Harold just shook his head ferociously, while Evans and the street vendor shared some silent laughter. With the change being enough for a good few more maize cobs, Evans knew where his next few snacks would be coming from. He winked at the woman, watching Harold take another large bite of the maize.

The woman leaned forward to poke the charcoal, and suddenly coughed loudly and violently over the other cobs still grilling on the brazier.

Harold screamed, spitting the maize in his mouth into his mask. He ripped off his mask to the sound of Evans's mocking laughter.

"Bro!" Evans roared between laughs. "You have no mask! You could get the..." he paused for emphasis and raised his fingers in quote marks before continuing in a passable impression of his twin – "CONVID!"

Harold spat out the rest of the maize and produced a bottle of antiseptic mouthwash from his jacket pocket. He sloshed a generous dose into his mouth and gargled loudly.

"Quick!" he yelled to Evans. "Hospital! We need to be tested! This woman could be sick!"

"Sick like yo brains, atase!" the shocked maize seller yelled at his rapidly retreating back.

7: THIS VERY SAME DAY

Unsurprisingly, presented with the choice of a visit to the COVID-19 test centre at Kafue General Hospital or a covert visit to the officially closed Sam's Tavern, Evans had chosen the latter. If he had contracted coronavirus, Evans mused, he would still have it after he had enjoyed a few beers. It wasn't going anywhere. And, if he hadn't contracted coronavirus, then all he would achieve by going to the COVID-19 test centre would be to waste time that could be better spent drinking. Evans's calm analysis did nothing to assuage Harold's fears, and in the end, Harold rushed off in a flurry of self-importance and irrational panic, while Evans knocked lazily on the locked door of Sam's Tavern.

"Go away" Sam's voice called from somewhere inside. "We are closed."

"But why?" Evans whined. "It is morning."

"We are on lockdown. Everybody knows this same thing."

"Aiii, exactly. That is why me I have come. I am asking to inspect the premises."

"Ohhhh, why didn't you say?" There was a loud metallic rattle as the door was unbolted and Sam peered out. Seeing only Evans, he nodded him in.

Evans looked around at the usual collection of drinkers. "Bwanji, ma inspectors. Ati shani?"

"This bar is closed," one replied. "We have checked, and it has been closed properly." He belched loudly and waved his empty bottle in the direction of Sam.

Taking his spot at the bar, Evans asked Sam where the girls were. "This bar only has men inspecting, how?"

"You can call yo' girls yo' self" Sam told him. Evans pulled out his phone, remembered his rather rash promise of buying the girls a pair of slippers each, and promptly returned it to his pocket again. "Mwandi," he sighed, "this bar is already too crowded. Just give me some one beer."

Evans stared unseeingly at his second "one beer." During his first "one beer" he had experienced a brief twinge of guilt at having left Harold to his own devices. He had tried to be helpful, by offering to get the keys and go and check on the hardware store on Harold's behalf, but for some reason Harold had been dead-set against that option. It was a very firm "no", that had been roared while his twin's face turned a peculiar shade, one that made Evans think that if Harold continued to get so wound up over little things like the security of his business, he would be visiting the hospital very soon anyway, albeit for a different reason.

The feeling of guilt grew. After all, Harold had just been trying to make sure that Evans was safe, and that he hadn't caught coronavirus, hadn't he? And Harold was blood. Grandfather would have wanted him to look after his twin. Perhaps he shouldn't be sitting here in Sam's Tavern at this precise moment in time. Perhaps he shouldn't have gone looking for Harold in the first place. Evans had brooded over these thoughts, realising that twinges of guilt and doom often seemed to arise during the first drink, but evaporate after two or three more, so he had ordered the second to see if the feeling continued.

Perhaps he would shortly receive a vision from Grandfather as to how he was supposed to resolve this dilemma.

As he nursed his second beer, Evans wondered how Harold was getting on at the hospital. He suspected that somewhere along the way the self-importance of his brother would meet the inflexibility of procedure and the two would have a stand-off of some variety. Evans knew that he was far more streetwise than his twin, and thought that perhaps he ought to go and help him. He knew only too well that the less compliant you were, the less a procedure would bend, and that the only ways to bend a procedure were through either charm or cash. As Harold was unlikely to dispense either, Evans was pretty sure that his twin would be at the hospital for quite some time, no matter how rapid the test claimed itself to be. Time enough, at least, for one more beer first. Maybe even two. No sense in rushing things, he really ought to give his brother a chance to prove himself first. Harold might come and find him here soon, and then Evans would have made the effort of getting up from the bar stool for nothing. That decided, Evans ordered another one more beer, and tuned-in to the gossip from his fellow health inspectors.

Harold was out of breath and in need of a seat by the time he reached the entrance to Kafue General Hospital. The hospital was a single-storey brick building, a mixture of colonial style red-brick and more recent concrete blocks covered in a healthy dose of plaster and fading regulation off-cream paint.

A guard stopped him as he walked through the open gate, and pointed to a grotty looking bucket and basin, with a small bottle of liquid hand soap beside it. "Boss, you have to wash hands."

Harold took a closer look at the state of the wash station and protested. "I have my own handi santitiza!" He waved the bottle proudly at the guard.

"Theliz rules. No washing, no going inside." The guard was adamant – and not just because he had been told in no uncertain terms what would happen to him if he slacked off on sanitising. His aunty was in the isolation ward in the same hospital, receiving oxygen therapy for COVID-19, and whether she would make it or not was currently the hot topic at home.

Harold sighed and complied, spending a brief three seconds giving the impression of washing his hands, before liberally covering his hands in his own sanitiser. He was still rubbing it into his hands as he walked into the hospital.

A handwritten sign for COVID-19 tests was stuck to the wall, pointing down a corridor. Harold turned in the direction shown, only to find himself at the end of a long queue. Those in the queue seemed to be attempting some form of social distancing, with variable sized gaps between individuals, or, in some cases, tight huddles of individuals, in a haphazard line.

The inconsistency rankled at his sense of propriety. This was not how one organised an orderly socially-distanced queue.

Putting the queue into some semblance of order was clearly his civic duty, and, if in doing so he happened to find himself at the front of the queue as a reward, well, that was quite alright with him.

He pulled his measuring tape out from his pocket and began measuring the distance between the two people in front of him. "Scuse, scuse" he nodded to the person at the end of the queue, a colourfully dressed young woman with long braided hair engrossed in another life on her cell phone, weaving his way around her. The young woman rolled her eyes and went back to her phone. Harold often seemed to have this effect on young women. Even his wife's niece was perpetually rolling her eyes in his presence, especially when he attempted to advise her on how to further her studies and develop her career. Harold usually took this to be a sign that his wife's niece was paying attention – after all, if she wasn't listening, she wouldn't know when to roll her eyes, would she? It was a reassuring thought, so the more she rolled her eyes, the longer he encouraged her– something she hadn't yet cottoned on to.

Harold took out his measuring tape and began measuring a metre from the eye-rolling young woman to the next person in the queue, a portly man, probably in his thirties, and dressed in the standard trousers, shirt and tie attire that literally screamed junior bookkeeper. Harold was very clear as to what a junior bookkeeper looked like – after all, he had so far fired around 20 of them, so many in fact that having worked at Harold's shop had become part of the template for any budding bookkeeper in the small town that Kafue was. He was pretty sure he had even fired this man at some point many years earlier, but, if so, it was probably better not to go there.

"What are you doing, man?" the man asked.

"I am checking to see that everyone in the queue is observing the correct social distance" Harold informed him, suddenly concentrating perhaps too obviously on his tape measure. "I want to make sure you are safe."

The man took a threatening step towards

Harold.

"No, please stay where you are! I've just finished measuring!" Harold complained. "Don't move after I have measured your distance."

"You are not the boss of me" the man growled. Yes, Harold had indeed fired this man many years earlier, at the start of his now flourishing career as a junior bookkeeper. Harold remembered him now. He had fired him because he tended to round up prices to the nearest whole number, whereas Harold liked prices to be exactly as the maths dictated. If a nail was going to be 23 kwacha 56 ngwee, then let it be 23 kwacha 56 ngwee. Why did it have to become 24 kwacha, or, worse, 23 kwacha 50 ngwee? "Who gave you the right to start bossing us around apa so? You are going to make me lose my place in this queue!"

"You are still at the same place in the queue" Harold announced, as he skirted around the next person, a timid looking lady, humbly dressed in a plain black top and a Catholic church chitenge around her waist. Harold peered back at the man triumphantly. "You see, you were in between these two women before I checked your distance, and you are still between them!"

There wasn't really much the man could say to that, so he settled for glaring at Harold instead. Harold, on the other hand, was now feeling quite pleased with himself, at least until he saw the next person in the queue.

Harold took a deep breath. He recognised her

only too well. In her forties, she was tall, smartly dressed in a business suit, with a very neat, short afro and a piercing glare that could wither the freshest of plants at about 50 paces. He recognised her because she was a regular customer in his shop, but a particularly difficult one. Whereas most of his customers trusted his advice, she was always extremely pedantic (and for Harold to describe someone as pedantic, it had to be a whole different level). On her last visit to the shop, she had come to buy a pack of nails, and insisted that Harold open and empty the pack to make sure that every single nail was the same size. This had been a lot of work, considering that she was buying a bulk pack of 100 nails. Harold decided that attempting to explain his actions to her was inviting trouble, so he opted for giving her a nervous giggle and a rather pathetic looking wave of his fingers, which earned him a snort of contempt, and he safely scuttled around her, letting out his breath once he was past.

Harold repeated this activity about a dozen times, using his measuring tape all the while, punctuating his activities with greetings, nods, and "am checking for social distance" by way of explanation, until finally the front of the queue was in sight.

All that stood between him and the pole position were a 70-something bald man and a young man dressed like he had only just got out of bed – in baggy clothes and trousers that were halfway down his backside, making sure that everyone knew just what colour of boxer shorts he preferred. For one tantalising moment, Harold was tempted to give the young man's trousers a hefty tug and pull them up to what he viewed as a more socially acceptable level, before it occurred to him that it was not only would breach his built-in social distancing rules but also probably result in an altercation that would delay him in getting to the front of the queue. So Harold left the young man's trousers where they were and jostled past the bald elderly man, who was standing in front of a traditionally-built nurse at the front of the queue. "What's wrong with you?" the man asked him.

"Nothing; that's why am in the priority queue! I get tested, I am fine, I go home! I can even test myself!"

"The only thing you are testing is my patience!" the man retorted.

Harold sucked his teeth. "I'll show you, old man." He turned to the nurse. "I'm ready!"

With a blank face and diffident attitude, she opened a door and pointed Harold through it.

8: JUST NOW

Harold found himself outside. He looked around in confusion, and then stormed back in. "What's the meaning of this?" he demanded angrily.

The traditionally-built nurse gave him a stare that would have a charging elephant reconsidering his life choices. However, Harold had several older sisters who were also traditionally-built in both appearance and temperament, as well as having been married to one for two decades, so he was unperturbed by a staring match with a large, grumpy woman.

"Well?" he repeated.

"I heard you say you were ready to go" she replied, feigning innocence.

"I'm ready to do the test!" he roared, loud enough to make the old man he had jumped in front of take several steps back, and even to make the young woman near the back of the queue look up from her phone. Dismissing the disturbance as a skirmish between a bunch of old people, the young woman returned to her cellular world, while Harold tried to contain himself. Honestly, how hard was it to be understood?

The nurse sighed and motioned to a different door. He didn't bother with a thank you and charged on through it.

9: MANJE MANJE (SOON SOON)

Harold found himself in a large rectangular room filled with posters about managing a healthy pregnancy. A large sign for antenatal classes dominated the room. He looked around and saw some curtained cubicles towards the end of the room. He stomped towards them, concerned that once again he might be being sent on a wild goose chase.

Harold entered the cubicle and found a lab assistant covered head to toe in protective gear sitting at a desk, busy with paperwork. He was quite pleased about this; this was someone who clearly knew how to santitize. And with the sign above a desk inside proudly stating *Rapid Test Centre*, he knew he could soon get out of the hospital and on with his day. Just as soon as the lab assistant stopped faffing around with the sheets of paper that littered his desk.

"Good afternoon" Harold announced in a loud voice, which made the man jump. At least it looked like a man to Harold. It was quite hard to tell from behind who lay underneath all that.

"Am coming, take a seat" he muttered in a muffled voice and waved his arm vaguely at a lopsided chair beside the table. From the looks of the chair, whose fabric covering proudly declared it to be a refugee from the 1970s, Harold suspected it had been hovering around a store room in the hospital for decades before finally having an opportunity for gainful employment when the pandemic arrived. He strongly suspected the same could also be said of the seemingly androgynous lab tech. However, for perhaps the first time that day, Harold simply did as he was told without arguing and sat down, realising that arguing with someone who might be about to stick something up your nose in the name of a lab test was probably not a great plan.

"Wait," said the muffle to Harold again, before turning to someone just out of sight and bellowing, "Ni bwela soon soon". Aha, thought Harold, it's a boy! He then paused and realised that this was perhaps a quite idiotic thought, and that clearly the number of posters he had seen along the way referring to the antenatal classes were getting to him. He had a big worry though, and it was already starting to niggle at him. "Soon soon" was such a wonderfully vague phrase, and it covered all sorts of sins against time keeping. In reality "soon soon" meant not soon but an indeterminately long version of the concept of "soon" that would have dictionary curators grinding their teeth and breaking down in floods of tears.

His twin, in particular, was very adept at this – especially, when it came to him paying back any borrowings. Any debt was always going to be paid "soon soon", and somehow, that particular point in time never seemed to arrive.

(Evans, interestingly enough, had a very clear idea of when "soon soon" was: it was a point in the future that would arrive, with a flourish, and when that time came it would perhaps be accompanied by the Lord himself. Evans had been told repeated in Sunday School as a child that he should be on his best behaviour because the Lord was coming soon – he had even had to learn a song about it – and so, for that reason, it was not worth worrying about the debts that were due "soon soon", because He was also coming soon, and thus the matter of unpaid debt would satisfactorily take care of itself. Evans was very proud of his faith, and would take great offence with anyone – including Harold – who impugned it by suggesting that his understanding of the gospel was incorrect when they suggested payment sooner than the day of the Lord's coming.)

Ten minutes later, Harold was starting to realise two things. Firstly, the chair was not nearly as comfortable as it had looked at first glance, having been assaulted by a wide range of behinds over the years and lost along the way whatever benefits to the occupant its creator might originally have envisaged. Secondly, the lab assistant's definition of "soon soon" was definitely closer to Evans's interpretation of time than Harold's.

He shuffled in the chair and decided that rather than sit there until the chair collapsed under him, he should perhaps be proactive, as was befitting to a man of his reputation, and go and hunt the lab technician down. However, this presented him with another dilemma. He had gone through a lot in order to get to his current point in the process as the next person to be tested, and he wasn't sure that he wanted to find himself having to renegotiate with the nurse, let alone the other people in the queue. If he wandered off, wouldn't he find this precious, albeit uncomfortable and tedious seat taken by someone else? He thought for a bit, before reaching into his pocket of his jacket for a pen and looked around for something to write on. Among the things on the desk that the lab technician had been shuffling around, was a blank sheet of paper. Harold liberally sprayed this with hand sanitiser before picking it up and writing *Reserved for Harold* on it in his flowery handwriting. He stood up, placed the sheet on the seat, and that matter dealt with, left the cubicle and wandered off down a corridor following signs for the lab.

After a few wrong turns Harold managed to find the lab only to be met with a locked door with a sheet of paper with *BACK SOON* scrawled on it in blue biro. "Soon," muttered Harold. "There is that word again." However, he also didn't trust diversionary messages, knowing full well that if he didn't lecture his staff in the morning, they would never get around to turning the sign he had hung on the door of his hardware shop from *Closed* to *Open.* He knocked a few times, and no answer was forthcoming.

Harold fidgeted a bit more, and then decided that on this occasion perhaps the sign was genuine, even if the sign writer's definition of soon was extremely unlikely to match his, so he would focus his attention on the hospital's reception desk. Surely, if anyone could find an errant lab technician, it should be the reception desk, the hub of the whole facility? Having reassured himself in advance, Harold set off to the reception desk, hoping that he wouldn't have lost his position in the cubicle and find himself having to re-join the queue.

Harold approached the reception desk at speed. The receptionist, a neat, short, slightly plump woman with a badge that pronounced her name to be Hope, was busy on a phone, chewing gum while she spoke to someone. Seeing how extensively her jaws appeared to be moving behind her mask, Harold was quite glad that it was sparing him a detailed view of how half-chewed gum looks. He fidgeted impatiently while waiting for her to finish, fishing around in his pocket for his beloved hand sanitiser. As he rubbed his hands together for perhaps the hundredth time that day, Harold caught snatches of Hope's side of the conversation: "Awe... sure? The committee? It is meeting tomorrow?"

She fidgeted with her long braids as she talked: to Harold's eyes this was a sign that something complicated was going on. Mercy always did that whenever she had a difficult decision to make. The discussion sounded really rather important, and, important as he was, he did think that perhaps a hospital committee arrangement was a significant matter, and deserving of a little patience on his part. He listened some more.

"Three hundred? And manje we have to buy our own chitenges? Awe this bride is asking too much..."

At this point Harold realised that the conversation was not about a critical hospital committee on sanitary methods, for example, but about a social committee to raise funds for a relative of Hope's wedding. "EXCUSE ME, MADAM" he roared, and she dropped the phone in fright.

"Yes, sir, what?"

"I have been waiting for an age!" Harold fumed. "First, queues, then the man doing your so-called rapid test disappears to do I don't know what with I don't know who I don't know where, and then I have to wait because you are too busy with some wedding committee to help your patients!"

"Sorry, sir" Hope said, standing up, smoothing down her skirt, and pushing her chair back against the desk.

Harold was almost speechless. "Where are you going?" he demanded.

"Sorry sir, I have gone for lunch." She strode off, leaving Harold in the company of her scent, and not much else. He mused to himself that with Hope having departed for lunch, the reception was no longer just metaphorically hope-less but now also literally so. This gave him some brief amusement, until he remembered why he had been standing there in the first place.

He was just about to start banging loudly on the desk when a well-manicured young lady with bright eyes, full cheeks, a large smile straining from behind her colourful chitenge mask, a cardigan several sizes too big for her slender frame and an even larger handbag strode up to the desk and, with much shuffling of the receptionist's chair, banging about and general ado, parked herself behind it. She rearranged her hair, rummaged in her handbag until her hand reappeared from its depths with a pen in it, and fixated her smile on Harold. "How can I help?"

Harold sighed heavily. Why was this so difficult? He took a deep breath and explained that he had been in the queue for the rapid test for coronavirus, and that having reached the front of the queue, and finally managed to get himself inside the cubicle for the test, the lab technician who was to administer the test had promptly disappeared – which, by the way, was the only time he had seen anything approaching rapid since arriving at the hospital – and had yet to return from wherever he had gone. He went on to tell her that he was a very busy man with important things to do, important places to be, and important people to see, and around here he just wanted to see one person, and that was the person to administer his test, and he wanted to see them immediately.

"No problem" she beamed at him, lifted the phone receiver from her desk and dialled. Harold's mood wasn't particularly improved by this. Generally, in his experience, when people said something was "no problem" they meant they didn't particularly care if the mission in hand succeeded or not.

She twiddled with the phone cable, tapping her nails on the desk as she did so. "They are not picking up." She smiled beatifically at him.

"So? Try again!"

She smiled even brighter at Harold, picked up the phone again, and dialled another extension. "Hallo, who is this?" A pause. "Ohhhh, how are you today?" Another pause. "How's home?"

Harold starts to understand what the beginnings of nuclear fusion might feel like. What on earth had the home life of the person on the other end of the phone got to do with finding a skiving lab tech? He understood the importance of niceties, but, really, sometimes it went far too far. Next the receptionist would be asking how the weather was that side, forgetting that they were in fact in the same building and less than 100 metres away from each other.

"Is Mulenga that side? No? Ah ha where has he gone, kanshi?" Another pause while a long explanation is proffered to the receptionist. At this point, Harold was imagining that the missing Mulenga had been captured by an escaped prisoner who, if there was any justice in the world, would be busy beating him over the head with a clock. The receptionist put down the phone, and eyed Harold warily. She opted for her prettiest smile. "I'm sorry sir, the lab tech will be back shortly. They want to make sure you have the right kind of test kit for a man of your importance." She smiled even harder. Harold knew this to be a complete lie but decided to give in and stomp off back to the testing cubicle.

Harold was really restless now. He was beginning to wonder if perhaps he had over-reacted after his experience with the maize seller, and, worse still, he was remembering where he had been going when he first met Evans in the street. It was, he thought, entirely possible that while he was sitting here waiting for someone who clearly didn't understand the concept of "rapid", the levels of stock in his hardware store were adjusting themselves. This could be a complete disaster – not just due to the financial impact to him personally, but for the good people of Kafue. How would they cope with a shortage of nails when they needed them if his staff had already unofficially distributed them to less than honest shoppers?

After what felt like an eternity, the lab tech finally reappeared, poking their head around the corner of the hospital privacy curtain to check if there was anyone waiting for a test. Seeing Harold, they stepped into the cubicle.

"About time, young man!" Harold said rudely. "You have no concept of time! I have been waiting for a long time! What kind of rapid is this?"

"Sorry sir," came a decidedly female voice from somewhere deep inside the safety outfit. "But ine am a woman."

"You were a man when you were here before!" said Harold, making matters worse. "Man or woman, you are taking too long. Maybe you took that time to have a sex change!"

Needless to say, this didn't help speed the process up. The lab tech sat down and told him very firmly to wait while she prepared the paperwork. She opened a fresh test kit and prepared to stick the swab up his nose.

This, for Harold, was more than a little unnerving. Here he was, seated on a chair that had seen better decades, never mind days, that felt like it could collapse at any moment, and advancing on him was an angry young woman who intended to stick a swab up his nose with, he feared, great ferocity.

And, indeed, great ferocity would have been an understatement. Involuntarily, Harold let out a very feminine squeal.

"You were a man when you were here before," she smirked. At least, it sounded like a smirk. It was impossible to tell under all that gear. "Your test will be ready in our concept of rapid time, sir."

A quarter of an hour later Harold was getting restless. That lab tech had got right up his nose, and not just in the physical sense. He had been told it was a rapid test, and to him, rapid should be defined as almost instantaneous. He left his space on the bench beside the old man in the waiting area for perhaps the tenth time in as many minutes and approached the desk, staffed by another, equally traditionally built nurse. "Well?" he demanded.

"Patience, please, sir," she replied.

Harold stomped back to the bench and sat down again. He was so keen to keep as much space as possible between himself and the old man that he ended up sitting perched on the edge of the bench, one buttock on, one off. It was uncomfortable, undignified, inelegant and definitely not befitting to a man of Harold's status in life – but it was still better than catching COVID-19 from a pensioner.

"I am here because of my daughter" the old man told Harold. "She lives in Manchester in England, do you know it?"

"Of course I know it," bristled Harold. "Do you think am from the village?" He pulled at his jacket. "This is finest Harris Tweed, sent by my uncle that side."

"Ohhhh. Kanshi it's nice. Me I thought it was salalula. Anyway," the old man continued, "my daughter works there as a nurse. She keeps telling me, 'daddy, you need to be taking this corona vilus seriously'. So, now, she told me, if I am not being serious and getting tested often, she will stop, you know." He rubbed his thumb and index finger together, indicating money. "So, am here." He chortled to himself.

A vendor was busy making his way round the waiting area, trying to flog his wares, which mostly consisted of a disconcerting combination of dog collars, toilet plungers, toothbrushes, and XXL boxer shorts. Street vendor offerings in Zambia were often like this, and one could while away a good many hours trying to wonder quite who would need all of their selection at one time, and why. The vendor spotted Harold's jacket and probably concluded that he must be a gullible man to have been persuaded into wearing it. He approached him with his wares outstretched. "Bwana, I have good deals."

"No", said Harold, rudely. He waved him away.

"Boss, I have the strongest toothbrushes. This toothbrush is so strong, that when you buy it, you had better go make a will so that when you die your relatives can keep using it."

"That is disgusting," said Harold, in a horrified tone. He got up from the bench to check for his results again.

"What about you, mudala?" the vendor asked the old man.

The old man just pulled down his face mask and gave the vendor a toothless grin. The vendor laughed and moved on to his next potential.

The nurse rolled her eyes as Harold hopped from one foot to the other impatiently, a movement that made him look like a toddler in urgent need of emptying its bladder. She shuffled around the envelopes on her desk, eventually selecting one and handing it towards Harold, who rudely snatched it straight out of her hand. He sprayed it liberally with hand sanitiser, hastily ripping open the envelope.

He slid the folded sheet out, his eyes catching sight of the print out above the fold:

RESULT: POSITIVE

"No! It can't be!" Harold ranted. "I santitize all the time, every day, every moment! See, I even santitised this!" He unfolded the rest of the sheet.

RESULT: POSITIVE

CONFIRMED STATUS: PREGNANT.
YOUR PREGNANCY: Next Steps.

Harold shredded the letter without reading any further, simultaneously turning from his usual dark chocolate colour to a strange purple, with the blood vessel on his forehead pumping away ferociously. "Nurse!" he roared. "What is the meaning of this nonsense! Are you trying to make a fool out of me?"

"No, I think you can do that without help," the old man quipped from behind him.

The traditionally built nurse attempted to look contrite. "Sorry, sorry, sir. I think there has been a mistake."

"Damn right there has! You've got the wrong bloody gender for a start! I'm not pregnant! If I was, I would be fat, angry, and cranky!"

The old man degenerated into a fit of giggles

interspersed by some heavy coughing.

The nurse shuffled some more papers around, and handed Harold another envelope, apologising as he sanitised it. "Sorry, sorry, sir. This is the right one."

"Are you sure?" Harold waved the still sealed envelope angrily, while spraying it liberally with sanitiser. "This could even just be an IQ test!"

"You needn't worry about it being positive then," the old man muttered.

Harold scowled in his general direction and ripped open the envelope.

RESULT: POSITIVE

"Again! More nonsense!" He shook the envelope and the sheet fell out onto the counter. "What's wrong with you people??" He shook his fist at the nurse, before realising she was staring at the results. Harold followed her gaze.

RESULT: POSITIVE

CONFIRMED STATUS: COVID-19 TESTED POSITIVE. ACTION: Immediate quarantine and admission required.

Harold was shocked. "No! It can't be! I santitize all the time, every day, every moment! Each time! I santitised this! I know how to santitize! No..." He was shaking as the nurse took him by the arm and led him towards the Isolation Ward.

"Bye bye," the old man called after him

cheerily, with a wave and grin.

10: MAILO (TOMORROW)

A combination of complaining loudly and handing over a large wad of cash had got Harold a private room at the far end of the hospital's COVID-19 isolation wing. He was pleased about this, at least. It just showed that if you made your feelings known clearly and firmly, you would get the treatment you deserved. It hadn't occurred to him that the sisters were more than happy to put him in the room farthest from the nurses' station, from which perhaps his bellyaching and complaining would at least be a little harder to hear. One of the nurses had even suggested locking the door to the room he was in, but in the end devotion to duty had put paid to that idea.

Getting Harold into the bed had been a mission in itself. To start with, he had insisted that nursing staff bring in clean bedding and make the bed while he watched. That done, he had proceeded to lather the bedding with his beloved "santitiza". That had been followed by an argument over whether or not he really needed to get fully undressed when this was clearly a chest and lung based disease. It had taken the Sister-in-Charge to come to the ward and explain in no uncertain terms that the mosquitoes hovering around the ceiling had bigger appendages than the one he was afraid of exposing, and that if he didn't cooperate she would remove the mosquito net and bed covers, undress him by force, and leave the mosquitoes to decide which part of his flesh was the most tender.

All that drama was now more than a day behind him, Harold was already getting bored. There was nobody to share his world views with, as he was not allowed visitors and the nurses felt that they had already had enough exposure to Harold and his opinions to last them a very long time.

He wheezed and shuffled himself on the bed. Hospital beds were not really designed for comfort. This he had concluded about two minutes after being ordered to lie down. He had been extremely careful, "santitized" everything he could (and then some), knowing his asthma made him vulnerable, and yet still, here he was, stuck in isolation.

A small wall-mounted TV in the corner sat on mute, perpetually tuned to a channel showing Mexican soaps; it appeared that a previous resident had made off with the remote, leaving Harold with no option – he couldn't leave the bed to fiddle with it, and the nursing staff had made it quite clear that the only changing they were responsible for was bed linen. Granted, it had taken him four attempts at calls on the emergency buzzer at different times of the day before they had managed to get the message through to him that that was not what the buzzer was for.

The last nurse to respond to his buzzer, a rather muscular looking male nurse this time, had waved a large bedpan in his general direction and had painted a rather vivid picture of what might happen if he kept buzzing for a channel change, and then had promptly switched the channel to this ludicrous selection of muted soaps as a form of mental torture. At least, it was for Harold. He had once, in his more romantic years, willingly volunteered to watch one with Mercy, before realising that no matter how strong his love for her was, it was better to show his love for her by granting her alone time to enjoy her Mexican soaps without his grumbled comments.

Harold coughed violently, his third or fourth coughing spree that morning. A doctor had been along to see him the day before, and from the depths of his (or her: he wasn't going to make that mistake twice) protective clothing had explained that Harold was being very closely monitored because he was at extremely high risk of deteriorating to needing oxygen therapy very shortly, as a result of his pre-existing asthma, and his blood pressure. Apparently his nurses had noted that seemed to shoot to astronomical levels the minute anyone spoke to him. As a result, he would be in this room for quite some days while they monitored him for his own good.

He was not quite as convinced as they were that this was for his own good. Indeed, he could think of dozens of reasons why the nation was suffering from him being locked up inside this unit, unable to do more than toddle to the bathroom and back with cables attached. There was quite some irony in the timing of this incarceration, he thought, as he had seen a banner announcing that Kafue's vaccine roll-out would begin shortly on a muted headline before the muscleman nurse had changed the channel on him. He gave up on his musings and went to sleep for a bit.

Harold, woken up by his own coughing, couldn't quite remember where he was. He had been having a glorious dream, one in which he had become President and, with his newly granted wide-sweeping powers, he had made Evans the state ambassador to the Tonga Islands. Zambia didn't have an embassy in Tonga; Harold had created one in as his first Presidential act in order to send Evans somewhere far away and remote. Given that in his dream he had been deciding this from the luxury of a Presidential bedroom, it was quite a shock to wake up and discover that he was not in fact relaxing in a comfortable bed with luxury linen but on an unfriendly hospital mattress with linen that had been starched to the texture of cardboard.

Harold looked around the shabby room in disdain. He really didn't understand why he was the one stuck in here, while his reckless twin had practically advertised himself as a COVID-19 host body and yet had somehow escaped. Life really wasn't fair. He had sanitised everything he touched, socially distanced, masked up – with three layers of masks for that matter – and still he had ended up in this ward, biding his time, wondering what would become of him. He turned – as much as the assorted equipment attached to him would allow – and faced the large, open window. The window was Harold's one source of pleasure in his little private ward – it had an open view, and he could see the Kafue River dawdling along in the distance. The river was blissfully unaware of coronavirus. The water would still churn the power turbines of Kafue Gorge dam; it would still feed the water intakes for Lusaka's water supply system; the hippos would still help themselves to the grass on the banks of the river; the crocodiles would still help themselves to the fish; and the witch doctors would still help themselves to the crocodiles. The river had behaved like that for millennia, and the fact that Harold was stuck in this room, hooked up to assorted monitors, looking out this window at it, would not change things one bit. It was almost humbling. Harold sighed.

There was a sudden scrambling noise outside the window; it was loud enough to make Harold remember the legends of times gone by and wonder if a hippo had come to life as a man and was on his way to turn Harold into a convenient snack.

The scrambling continued, and a pair of hands appeared on the window ledge. "Whaaaaaat...?" Harold was startled.

Bit by bit, a head slowly appeared over the window ledge and a grinning Evans peered in.

"I should have known", said Harold, weakly. He sighed heavily as Evans laboriously pulled himself over the window ledge, landing in the ward with a thud. Evans stood up, dusted himself off, and looked around.

"Are you crazy?" Harold said. He laboured over the words. "You can't be in here! You'll get sick!

"Awe, bro, I am so safe. I don't get sick, ever! Even when we was small."

"Be serious, Evans. You never santitize! You never wear your mask properly! You could be asymptomatic!"

"I'm telling you, bro, there is nothing wrong with me. I have common sense!"

"You're asymptomatic of that too!" Harold snorted.

Evans looked at Harold, and for approximately three seconds actually felt sorry for him. "So this thing was real, te?"

Harold nodded, and spoke in a sombre manner. "You could have this convid too, you know."

"Awe, no", Evans laughed. "Me, I am very fine. I came to check on you. So I go tell your madam how you are."

The panic was clear on Harold's face. "No! Don't go near her! You'll take this infection. You need to santitize!"

"No problem, bro, no need."

Harold coughed violently. "No, I forbid it, iwe

Evans..." Harold's coughing worsened, becoming more pronounced and extreme. This set off an alarm on one of the monitors he was attached to.

The sound of footsteps approaching down the corridor was enough to make Evans give his twin a mock salute and dive out the window, making his escape just as the Sister charged into the room.

Evans dropped on to the grass outside and ran around the corner of the hospital building. As a getaway route, this had been foolproof when Evans had scouted it out earlier. However, he had not known about the planned delivery of vaccines in a light truck, nor had he known about the delivery driver's tendency to take corners at top speed. He had always wanted to be a rally driver and, sadly, careening about delivery bays at breakneck speed was the closest he got to fulfilling his dream.

And so it was that the unfortunate Evans ran head-first into the grill of the vaccination delivery truck. It is sufficient to say that the truck fared better than Evans did.

Her eyes full of tears, Mercy peered through the blinds into the isolation ward. She could see her husband's twin, Evans, lying unconscious. But why was Harold's bed empty? Her eyes followed the line of the cables from the oxygen tank and came to rest on Harold waving his measuring tape around. Even as he struggled to breathe, he was trying to make sure there was a least a metre between himself and Evans.

11: MAILO (LATER)

The gentle morning light was filtering through the acacia trees in the graveyard as the caretaker finished loading dirt into his wheelbarrow. He paused, leaned on his shovel, and looked at the two grave markers that stood solemnly in front of him.

Chiselled into the first one was:

HERE LIES HAROLD.
TAKEN BY THE DISEASE.
12 August 2021.

And the other stone, a twin as they were in life, read:

HERE LIES EVANS.
TAKEN BY THE VACCINE.
12 August 2021.

The caretaker mopped his brow with a dusty handkerchief and removed Harold's measuring tape from his pocket. He knelt down and measured the distance between the two freshly dug graves.

The metre apart confirmed, he rolled up the tape and placed it gently on Harold's grave.

GLOSSARY

This glossary is intended to be contextually relevant rather than linguistically accurate, and for that reason I apologise for any errors that may exist. I will fix them mailo.

Amapha chilichonse – everything

Apa – here

Ati – what

Ati bwanji? – literally, what, how – depending on context it can either be a how's it going? Or what the hell?

Atase – an insult. The less said here the better, perhaps.

Awe – (pronounced ahhh-way) no.

Beer – used indiscriminately locally as a generic term for bottled alcoholic beers and lagers; Evans would probably actually be drinking a lager rather than a beer.

Bwanji – howdy, an informal version of *muli bwanji?* which means *how are you?* In the context Evans uses the phrase, it is a greeting that doesn't necessarily require a reply, although it's generally considered polite to respond.

Chitenge – a stretch of wax printed and dyed cotton fabric, usually with bright patterns, typically used as a wrap around a woman's waist and legs. Used to refer to both the item once worn and to the fabric before cut/at point of purchase. For example, chitenge fabric might be bought in a six metre stretch for three ladies planning to wear the same style to a kitchen party, and then cut into three wraps – which they may make (or get a local tailor to make) a full dress from. A number of talented Zambian (and African for that matter) fashion designers use chitenge as the base material for their creations.

Kachasu – an illicit alcoholic brew distilled from maize

Kulibe – nothing

Kwacha/Ngwee – Zambian currency. 100 ngwee gives you 1 kwacha.

Ine – me/I

Lelo – today

Mailo – yesterday, tomorrow or some unspecified point in the future that is not today, depending on the context. Mailo can also be used as a "see you" phrase, without necessarily really meaning it.

Manje – now; but generally used as manje manje when used as a reference to a point in time. However, it is not really now as a stickler like Harold would see it. It can refer to any moment in time from this instant to a time within the day – it very much depends on who said it and what they were talking about when they said it.

Mudala – old man. Can be used respectfully or disdainfully, depending on context.

Muzungu – European. Used to refer to any Caucasian.

Mwandi – an expression of shame, empathy, pity or a literal sorry; sometimes used as a word in place of a heavy sigh. Context is important.

Tiye – slang version of tiyende: let's go.

Yo' – an urbanised slang version of *your,* where the latter half of the word is dropped.

AFTERWORD

Evans and Harold can be found anywhere, two very different reactions to the pandemic. From the overly cautious to the brash reckless, from attempts at draconian legislation to quite literally throwing political parties in the midst of a lock-down, they can be found anywhere in the world. They are not any more prevalent in Zambia: I simply chose to set it here because this is home, and locations are either fictitious, heavily fictionalised or used fictitiously (or all three at once for that matter). Actually, *used farcically* might be a better term.

Thankfully, most of our citizens are not like our dear twins, and have embraced the pandemic with the patient, gentle philosophy and good humour that so endears this land to my heart. And to the front-liners in this nation, often battling in very trying circumstances, without the luxuries of billions of dollars in healthcare procurement, I simply offer respect and thanks. You deserve that, and more.

Thank you to the many long-suffering friends and acquaintances here in Zed who I tested lines on... you didn't really deserve it, Ziko, Gift, Stan,

Camilla Hebo-Buus, my editor Hugh Barker and to mum, dad and Tracy for the additional whisperings of grammar.

Finally, this wouldn't have happened without my better half, who gives me a reason to believe.

ABOUT THE AUTHOR

Jonathan H Elliott

Scottish-born Jonathan H Elliott was raised in Lusaka, Zambia, where he lives, spending his time writing, being sarcastic, and - every now and then - doing something useful.

Printed in Great Britain
by Amazon

84650689R00078